VERTICAL WORLD V

DOWN FOR AIR

BY BRIAN CRAWFORD

EPIC Escape

An Imprint of EPIC Press
abdopublishing.com

Down for Air
Vertical World: Book #3

abdopublishing.com

Published by EPIC Press, a division of ABDO, PO Box 398166, Minneapolis, Minnesota 55439. Copyright © 2019 by Abdo Consulting Group, Inc. International copyrights reserved in all countries. No part of this book may be reproduced in any form without written permission from the publisher. Escape™ is a trademark and logo of EPIC Press.

Printed in the United States of America, North Mankato, Minnesota.
052018
092018

Cover design by Christina Doffing
Images for cover art obtained from iStockphoto.com
Edited by Gil Conrad

Library of Congress Cataloging-in-Publication Data

Library of Congress Control Number: 2018932903

Publisher's Cataloging in Publication Data

Names: Crawford, Brian, author.
Title: Down for air/ by Brian Crawford
Description: Minneapolis, MN : EPIC Press, 2019 | Series: Vertical world; #3
Summary: With their power plant destroyed, the Ætherians send a reconnaissance group down to Ætheria to investigate the disaster. While below, they encounter Aral, a sixteen-year-old Cthonian—the only person left alive after the Cthonians' botched attack on the Ætherian power plant. But when Aral realizes that Rex Himmel is related to an Ætherian asylum-seeker living among the Cthonians, Rex understands that Aral might be the connection he needed to rebuild his broken family.
Identifiers: ISBN 9781680769135 (lib. bdg.) | ISBN 9781680769418 (ebook)
Subjects: LCSH: Nuclear warfare--Fiction--Fiction. | Survival--Fiction--Fiction. | Revolutions--Fiction--Fiction. | Science fiction--Societies, etc--Fiction | Young adult fiction.
Classification: DDC [FIC]--dc23

This series is dedicated to Debbie Pearson.
Thank you for everything.

ONE

SCREAMING PANDEMONIUM WRACKED THE Ætherian archipelago, a group of twenty-four floating islands six miles above Cthonia's surface.

As soon as Ætheria's Power Works building and the entire Proboscis plummeted through the broiling, toxic Welcans cloud below, the dozens of gawkers on the adjacent islands exploded into a run, pouring away from the islands' edges. Some darted for their homes. Some disappeared into the tunnels connecting the windswept buildings. Some stumbled backwards, unable to move. For the eight hundred years of its existence, Ætheria had never suffered anything even remotely similar to the disaster that now faced the cloud dwellers. Because everyone wore UV goggles, their full expressions were hidden. But their gaping and screaming mouths said what their eyes couldn't: they feared their world was coming to an end.

Standing at the edge of Bernuac HQ, sixteen-year-old Rex Himmel worked his way backwards into the Ætherian Cover Force training building, which sat only ten yards away from where he'd been standing. For the first time in his life, he felt that Ætheria was in danger. Ætheria—an archipelago of twenty-four floating islands that sustained two thousand people above the clouds. Ætheria—a city consisting of massive manufactured clumps of ground held aloft by thousands of thin, stratoneum poles stretching all the way to Cthonia six miles below. Ætheria—where people had overcome a life of depleted oxygen, intense ultraviolet rays, and interminable high winds through clusters of tear-drop-shaped houses, hamster-cage-like transit tubes in between buildings, and Zipp lines connecting one island to the next. Ætheria—where farming and manufacture had been sustained for hundreds of years, all thanks to the Ætherians' ingenuity in protecting plants and livestock from the harsh elements. Ætheria—whose massive Proboscis tube had drawn water, cthoneum gas, and carbon dioxide from Cthonia to sustain life and generate electricity on Ætheria's most important island: Tátea.

Tátea—whose Power Works had just been destroyed by an unseen attack from far below. An attack that had killed Rex's foster dad, leaving him an orphan.

His ears ringing from the howling wind and the rising and falling screams, Rex headed back toward the Bernuac HQ building. Even though he'd been wearing his highly insulated and ultralight AeroGel suit outside, the sudden absence of wind and the insulation provided by the ACF training headquarters flooded him with warmth. He pushed through the main hatch and hurried down the winding transit tube leading into the building's heart. When he stepped into the training room he'd gotten to know so well just days before, he did a double take: the lights were back on. When the attack had occurred, the electricity had been cut; and now that Ætheria's only Power Works had been destroyed, there was no way for power to be generated and sent to the other twenty-three islands. *What was going on?*

When he stepped in, Rex had half-expected Bernuac HQ to be overflowing with many more people than before, when he'd come back up from the Proboscis. He expected not just ACF members, but normal Ætherians who'd come for answers. It was, after all, the Ætherian Cover Force's official role to "ensure the safety and welfare of all Ætherians," at least according to the badge they all wore on the center of their chests. But when he stepped into the training room, he saw only two dozen or so scouts huddled together on one side. *Where had everyone else gone?* He blinked at the lights and stepped in. Heads turned. Many were the same faces as before, but he only knew Yoné and Protector Challies among those who had gathered.

"Rex!" Yoné cried, breaking away from the group and running over. Before Rex could react, Yoné had thrown her arms around him and squeezed. Her grip was tight—bordering on painful—but filled with emotion.

"Can you believe it? Can you believe it?" she muttered, her lip quivering. The two locked eyes. Rex sensed she was trying to communicate with her gaze much more than words would allow . . . at least here, where others were listening.

"My dad was on there. My foster dad, I mean. On Tátea . . . " Rex's voice faltered. His throat stung. Even though he'd only met Yoné three days ago, and even though she was ten years older than him, he felt a painful urge to bury his head in her neck—not in any romantic way, but more like a child seeking comfort from his mother. Maternal comfort: this was something he'd never known, not since his own mother had left him as a baby.

Yoné took him in her arms once more.

"I'm so sorry. Oh, Rex, I'm so, so sorry."

He felt her hand rubbing his back, soothing him. Rex took a deep breath and pulled back.

"Both of my parents are gone," he said. He bit his lip and looked into Yoné's eyes, as if she could provide answers. She held his gaze, her mind racing with what she knew about Rex but was forbidden to reveal. *If only you knew,* she thought, *if only you knew . . .*

"I wish I had the right words," she finally said, "but . . ."

"There are no right words," he interrupted. "I'm sixteen. What's going to happen? To me? To all of us?"

"Look, let's take things one step at a time. I'll watch after you here. But later . . . " her voice trailed off.

Wanting to change the subject, Rex glanced around the room, his eyes settling on the ceiling.

"How do you—" he paused, raising his hands to point at the lights. "How is there electricity in here? The Power Works . . . the Proboscis . . . what are we . . . "

"There are backup generators," she said, eager to talk about something other than Rex's family. She stepped back and dropped her arms to her sides. "They're not common knowledge. And they're only on certain buildings: Ætherian Council buildings and the community centers. And we have water reserves, too. But," she ran her hand through her hair and looked around, a worried look crossing her face, "just enough for two weeks."

"What about food?"

"About two weeks as well. In each island there's a Larder—it's like a big closet under the surface with extra supplies: food, water, oxygen, SCRM masks . . . that sort of thing. It's the same place the maintenance teams can rappel down Ætheria's support wires for maintenance. But as far as all this is concerned, we're going to have to do something. Fast."

Rex nodded, a pang of fear coursing through him. The community centers were large buildings at the centers of most islands. Kids usually spent more time there than teens or adults. They were places where you could play games, run around inside without freezing, and in a few, swim in pools formed into hollows in the floating, man-made islands. Since he'd turned thirteen three years ago, Rex had only gone to one because he'd been invited to some event: a birthday party, a wedding . . . Even when kids did go there, very few of them actually played. Without supplemental oxygen, any effort beyond a brisk walk would make you lightheaded. Push yourself too hard and you risked hypoxia and unconsciousness. Now that Rex was older, he'd spent more time between school and his school's recreation center, which was more for teens. Even there, he went more to hang out or be away from his foster dad, who was never home that much anyways.

"There are generators in the community centers?" Rex asked.

Yoné nodded. "Yes. With the power cut between islands, we can't transmit messages anymore to non-Council or non-ACF. For us, the Trackers are enough." She tapped the smooth watch-like device strapped onto her wrist. Rex looked down at his own Tracker, which was clamped around his right wrist—his nondominant hand. "For normal Ætherians, members of the ACF are physically going from house to house to get people to come set up camp there."

"Camp?" Rex furrowed his brow. "Why?"

"Without heat, the houses are going to be deep freezers in less than twenty-four hours. Not to mention there's no water anywhere but in the Larders, and only ACF can access those. Even if there were water service to homes, the pipes are going to burst. The water will freeze. That's certain. No electricity, no way to heat the pipes. How do you think we've been pulling it off all these years?"

Of course, he thought. His mind was clouded by a mixture of fright, shock, and sorrow. Until that day, he'd never had any need to think about the logistics of how Ætheria worked. Just like good health: you only appreciate it when it's gone.

"Two weeks?" he said, looking up. His eyes wandered to the group of ACF scouts and troops who had resumed talking to each other. "But why aren't there more people here?"

"That's just it," Yoné said. "We've only just started sending people out to round everyone up. *That's* why there's only a few of us here. I think a lot of the people who were involved in our Ausculting mission ran home to find their families. After the attack, I mean. And yes, two weeks."

"But what do we do in that time? How can we survive without water? Without electricity? Oh, my God . . . "

Before Rex could become too paralyzed with

fear, Yoné snatched him by the sleeve and pulled him over to the growing group. Men and women looked up and nodded. He glanced around, only now able to see everyone's faces. At the other end of the huddle stood Deputy Head Schlott, the commander of the Ætherian Cover Force. Schlott had been the one to welcome the new recruits to the ACF just a few days before. Since his recruitment, training, and assignment as an ACF Auscultor, Rex had never spoken with Schlott beyond just a few words in passing and in gatherings. Schlott had recognized Rex during one of their first training assemblies, but that was it. A commanding aura surrounded her, almost as if her very being exuded power. Just by the way she held herself and by the way her darting, piercing eyes assessed every molecule within her sight, Rex felt he would be able to pick Schlott out of a crowd as one of Ætheria's most powerful people—even if she'd been wearing a normal AeroGel suit. Aside from her demeanor, she was also the only person in the room wearing an oxygen canister on her back. Connected to her nose via a small, transparent tube, the canister was a clear marker of official status in Ætheria—only members of the Ætherian Council or the High Command were allowed oxygen. Everyone else had to adapt—hypoxia or not.

"Deputy Head Schlott, all, this is Rex Himmel, sixteen."

Schlott stopped and looked at Rex.

"Yes, I remember you," she said. "I know who you are." As she spoke, Schlott's oxygen canister clicked and hissed with each inhale. Rex felt a chill at Schlott's words. So many people in the Ætherian High Command claimed to know who he was. But why?

"Rex might be young," Yoné continued, "but he was with me in Unit Alif when we went down the Proboscis." She paused and lowered her eyes. "His dad was head of Energy and Survival. Franklin Strapp." At these words, Rex thought he heard several gasps behind him. "Unfortunately his dad was on Tátea in the Power Works when . . . " she paused.

"Rex," Schlott stepped forward and placed her right hand on Rex's left shoulder. He looked up and met her gaze, which was fierce and comforting at the same time. "I am so sorry. This attack has opened a new chapter for Ætheria." She stepped back to her place in the circle and continued talking, now letting her eyes scan everyone present. "Yes, a new chapter. We are writing history. Our first estimates place the human loss at a few hundred, though we're not sure. As you can imagine, one Ætherian life lost is too many. Many of us knew someone who was over there. And your poor father . . .

"But," Schlott took a deep breath and drew herself up to an impressive height. As she spoke, Rex had the impression she was reading from a script. "Despite our fear and sorrow, we cannot allow ourselves to be beaten down. Nearly a millennium ago, our forefathers built up this complex to escape the environment down below on Cthonia. They never would've succeeded without courage, grit, and determination, especially in this environment. But they succeeded. And now . . . now that we are faced with a challenge similar only to our world's creation all those years ago, we have only one choice: to accept the challenge."

The scouts and troops nodded, their eyes fixed on Schlott.

"Shortly after the attack, I was able to reach Head Ductor Leif in his compound. We discussed briefly what must happen. And what we determined—without much discussion—was that we as a society have two tasks ahead of us.

"First: an immediate reconstruction of the Proboscis, with all its integral parts. As you may know, Islands Twenty-Three and Twenty-Four to the north contain Ætheria's principal factories for the production of all parts necessary to maintain our existence. Replacement parts exist—they have for centuries. We have just sent word to mobilize teams of workers to begin repair immediately, which, according to our calculations, should be completed in two months."

"Two months?" Rex blurted out. "Sorry, Deputy Head," he mumbled. Schlott nodded with a suppressed smile.

"Don't worry about it," Schlott said. "I know what you're thinking. The repair time puts us under the gun against our generator, water, and food reserves. And those will last for just two weeks. I get it. The clock is ticking. We will have to ration strictly to survive.

"But," her voice became stern, "the second goal is just as important, if not more important, than the first. We have been infiltrated and attacked. Those Cthonians have been sending up spies, and now they have launched an unprovoked attack on Tátea's Power Works, the beating heart of our civilization. I personally cannot think of anything more cowardly or heinous.

"So here's the point. If we do not secure the

Proboscis and our world, then our very existence will live under the threat of another attack from people who clearly have no sense of morality. And so, at the same time our teams are repairing the Proboscis, we are mobilizing the entire ACF—all two hundred recruits."

"Mobilizing?" Rex asked.

"We have to go down and make contact. Make contact and restore our water."

TWO

OVER THE NEXT HOUR OR SO, MORE AND more ACF scouts filed into the room. As their number increased, Rex could also feel the nervous energy grow. Worried faces betrayed the Ætherians' fear, rapid-fire conversations revealed their uncertainty, and the tightened features of Deputy Head Schlott and the other Protectors and members of the High Command conveyed anger and a sense of urgency.

When the room had reached near capacity, Schlott walked to the front of the room and stepped onto the speaker's platform.

"ACF!" As if on cue, Schlott's voice boomed through the stentrophones, causing the assembled scouts to turn and face the front of the room. There was a rustle of cloth and scuffle of feet as the scouts turned. Rex looked up.

"We are going to call roll," Schlott said, lifting a clipboard that Challies had passed to her at chest level. "Report when you hear your name."

She's not wasting any time, Rex thought. His body tingled with a mixture of terror and anticipation.

Schlott read out the names. Over the next few minutes, a chorus of "Present!" echoed back. Rex noticed the names were not ordered alphabetically. He wondered if they had been organized by age.

Only three or four names went unanswered. Each time this happened, Schlott paused, looked down at her clipboard, and called again, her voice growing more impatient through the stentrophones. After the third call, she whispered to Protector Roman or Protector Challies, who wrote something down on a small pad and then darted out of the room, returning seconds later. Rex wondered where the missing recruits could've been. At home? In one of the community centers? Or maybe they too had been on Tátea, or even in the doomed Power Works?

With roll call completed, Schlott raised her hand. "Unit Alif, in line and follow me! To Island Twenty-Three! I'll explain when we get there!" Schlott turned her back to the group and the Unit fell into two meandering lines of sixty. Unit Alif—this was the group Rex was in when he'd gone down the Proboscis.

"Island Twenty-Three?" Rex turned to Yoné, who fell in line next to him. "Isn't that one of Ætheria's warehouses Schlott just mentioned?"

"Yeah, sure is. About five miles away. North."

"Why are we going there, do you think? Isn't that where they make replacement parts for the Proboscis and whatnot?"

"Sure is," she said. "But I suspect there's something else."

Just fewer than two hours later, the scouts from Unit Alif gathered at the entrance of a bulbous, gray building that filled the expanse of Island Twenty-Three. At the northernmost edge of Ætheria, the island looked like a massive, five-story-high mushroom floating in the sky, with only a ten-yard lip of pathway around its perimeter. Rex had never been this far north. Just as Tátea had been, Islands Twenty-Three and Twenty-Four were off-limits, accessible only to members of the High Command and the Ætherian Council. Only they held a special Nanokepp Card that granted them access to the most sensitive islands in the archipelago, and the most secure buildings.

The group collected on the perilous lip outside of the structure. They huddled in close to the walls, avoiding the island's edge, which, unlike most of the islands in Ætheria, did not have a protective rail to prevent falls. The stratospheric wind howled around the group who, from a distance, looked like a small group of penguins huddled together against the Antarctic cold.

Once everyone was accounted for, Schlott pushed her way through to the building's entrance. She withdrew a Nanokepp Card from her uniform's front left pocket and held it against a small magnetic pad to the right of the door. A glowing red light flashed green and the door unbolted and lifted.

"Everyone inside!" she bellowed, waving the squadron in. Huddling next to Yoné, Rex shuffled his way inside.

Once Unit Alif had entered, the door slid closed with a ponderous crash.

Rubbing his hands to warm them, Rex walked with the others as they followed Schlott to the center of what seemed to be a massive holding area or meeting space. While the center of the building was hollowed out, all around stood hundreds of massive shelves stocked with every kind of metal, plastic, or electric part imaginable: wires, pipes, insulation, sheet metal, stratoneum alloy, nuts, bolts, screws, tools, grapples, ropes, harnesses, welding materials, and silver, glistening hardware as far as the eye could see.

Rex stood on his tiptoes and looked around. From what he could tell, this was just a huge storage facility. *Perhaps the actual manufacture of parts is on Island Twenty-Four?* he wondered, settling back down onto his feet.

When Schlott reached the middle of the warehouse, she turned and faced the group. Before she had finished moving, two men and two women had appeared from the stacks of shelves and materials with clipboards. Wearing dark blue overalls stained with grease, they clearly worked in the warehouse, and they seemed to have been expecting Schlott. As the five whispered to each other, the employees took hurried notes and then trotted off to different areas of the building. They moved with purpose, as if Schlott had just sent them to retrieve something. As they disappeared among the shelves, Rex noticed that dozens if not hundreds of other employees teemed about the warehouse's stores. Each held a clipboard, and each was frenetically scanning the shelves and removing items—some small, some massive, requiring four or five people to wrangle them. The employees were carrying the collected objects to the edge of the warehouse's clearing, where they slowly rose to form a wall of manufactured materials behind Schlott.

Rex wiggled his way forward through the group until he reached the front row of what had become a semicircle. Schlott stood at the center and faced the squadron.

Now that he had an unobstructed view, Rex noticed a network of metal rails that crisscrossed the floor and twelve strange objects lying in a line to Schlott's right. The objects, each a little larger than what Rex imagined to be a large coffin, looked like illustrations he'd seen as a child of giant butterfly cocoons. They were smooth and shiny, and the exterior was layered in texture, like scales on a glistening brown chrysalis. But unlike coffins, the pods did not lay flush on the ground. Rather, they lay tilted to one side, as if some protuberance on the back kept them from lying flat. A perfect seam divided the pods in half along their equators. As Rex scanned the bizarre structures, he was reminded of the black pods that had been found on the spies. Had these chrysalis-coffins also come up from below?

"Unit Alif," Schlott began. "Less than four hours ago, our society was attacked. Behind me you see that our workers are assembling the parts necessary to repair the Proboscis and restore water and electricity to Ætheria. I have already told you the time pressure that we are under to get this done and get it done right.

"But as for *you*," she pointed at the group, "*you* I brought here because all of you have been down the Proboscis and you have seen firsthand what the Cthonians were building down there—those tents. Because you know more than any of us, because you have *seen* what the Cthonians are doing, we now need you to go down again.

"These," she paused, pointing at the chrysalis-coffins, "are technically inspection descent pods. Whenever we've needed to go down to check the underside of the islands, or if ever we've had to inspect the stratoneum stilts, guy wires, and their foundations that hold up Ætheria, we've used these.

"As you can see, each is a little larger than one person. On the back," she leaned down and rotated one of pods over, revealing a series of latches and metal grips on the backside that protruded about six or seven inches. These had been what had kept the pods from lying flat. "These," Schlott pointed, "we clip on to the guy wires that help support the stilts and the islands. Some of you have used these." She let the cocoon roll back into place and stood. Rex noticed a few knowing nods from around the room.

"Using those, we clip the pods onto the guy wires with one of you in them, and then the pods slide down to Cthonia at a controlled rate. When you went down yesterday, it would've been much easier to use these, but we needed you to look *in* the Proboscis—which the Cthonian spies had been coming through. There was no other way.

"So right now, our first goal is this: We are going to send twelve of you down immediately in just as many pods through this hatch that leads to the bottom of this island and to the main guy wire supporting the stratoneum struts." Schlott pointed off to the side of the warehouse, where a lone trapdoor marred the floor with a series of latches and hinges. From where the squadron stood, a series of rails led away, rising slightly before dipping toward the latch.

"Because you've gone down as an Auscultor before, the only difference now is that you'll be spared the effort of having to climb up and down the Proboscis. But now, we need you to go straight to Cthonia and see whoever is down there. We have to make contact, see if there are any survivors, or both. But this time you'll be armed with one of these."

She walked off to the right of the line of pods where several tables held dozens of black devices. She picked one up. Even though Rex was now in the front row, he stood on his toes to see. Schlott turned toward the group, holding what looked like some sort of black drill or pistol. Rex immediately recognized the device as the weapon Protectors Challies and Roman had used on him when they'd arrested him earlier. The sight of the thing made Rex wince from the memory and clench his jaw in what he still felt was unfair treatment by the ACF.

"These Stær guns," Schlott continued, "are capable of incapacitating twenty persons at once. Their operation is simple: point at your target and pull the trigger. A blast of ten charges fly out to a distance of up to fifty yards and at a spread of forty feet. Anything they hit gets a charge of one hundred thousand volts. That usually produces instant but nonlethal paralysis. Of course," she set the Stær gun back down, "depending on how healthy the person is who gets the charge, it can stop the heart cold. Death would result."

A murmur swept through the scouts. Rex felt a chill. He was going to have to use one of these weapons? How? He'd never held any sort of weapon in his life. And he'd had no chance to practice. What if he messed up and misfired, shot himself or shot one of his teammates? Had the others received training with these guns? Had they already shot them? Was Rex being set up for failure? It was ridiculous to be thrown into this so unprepared, and with recruits much older than he.

Rex looked around at the others. They all nodded knowingly, as if using a Stær gun were second nature. But Rex? He felt like he was being sent on a suicide mission, apparently just so someone in the Ætherian Council could make a point about his being "different." But who?

"There is one thing." Schlott interrupted Rex's thoughts as if sensing that his worry was spinning out of control. "We hope that you won't need these. They are a precaution, period. For those of you who have gone down as Auscultors, your goal now is first to go down and assess where the explosion and attack occurred. Gather what evidence you can, take pictures, make notes, and hopefully find survivors. You will have enough water and supplies in the pods for a week out, but really we don't know how much time you'll need.

"But more than that, you need to find out who did this: where they live, how they live, and why they'd even do this to us. Because we will engage them. They are the ones who have attacked us. We've done *nothing* to them. Even if you need to explore away from the descent pod landing site, you need to look around—look around and get answers.

"But right now, it is not your job to engage unless attacked. Your job is to gather information and then return with any reconnaissance that you can. For the other half of you, your job will be to secure the Proboscis's foundation site so that construction can continue uninterrupted. In other words: make sure there are not hostile elements in the way.

"Go down, see what you can see, and come back with a report. After that we'll restock and send another group down to stand guard until the Proboscis is complete."

"Deputy Head Schlott?" a scout raised his hand off to the left.

"Yes?" Schlott asked.

"How do we know no one is down there waiting for us?"

Schlott nodded as if thinking, "Good question. Well," she began, "you'll remember the only way we can know what is happening below the Welcans cloud is to physically go below the cloud. It is made of fermionic lithium, after all, which is impervious to any radio, infrared, Doppler, or X-ray signals we may send down.

"So to answer your question: we *don't* know what's down there. To keep us covered, we're going to have to wait for a storm, which is forecast for tomorrow evening. And we can see this from above. Those are not that uncommon; and thunder, lightning, and acid rain should hide you from any of those Cthonians who might be down there. Which brings us here. We are just over five miles away from the collapse site of Tátea's Power Works, so if we can send you down in the cover of a storm at night, and if you are just as far away from them horizontally as we are now vertically, then your chances of going unnoticed are good. Before, we could've also gone down the Proboscis to look as you did; each island's underground Larder also contains a hatch that allows us to rappel down the guy wires from a harness. During a storm, that would be deadly, and you would be exposed to any unfriendlies down there. So now, going by descent pod is our only practical way. I know it's dangerous, but again, we have no other choice.

"Of course," she sighed, "not everything is foolproof. Which is why each pod has this." She stepped toward one of the pods, opened its cover, and pointed to a large blue button on the side. "If you get down there and see there's trouble, you press this. Pod shoots back up, and we know right away not to send anyone else down. Also, you each will be wearing a smaller pack on your back. In addition to containing your supply of oxygen, a headlamp, four liters of water, and food, it will have vitals monitors connected to each of your chests, as well as radio transmitters. You won't be able to transmit until you get below the Welcans cloud, and then you'll be able to talk to each other. But if your vitals drop to dangerous levels and you are incapacitated, the descent pods will come back up one at a time, automatically. And they'll come back not based on which pod you were actually in, but which is higher up on the guy wire—because they all go down on the same wire. That's how we'll know you're in life-threatening trouble, and then we'll send someone down to help. It's not ideal, but it's the only way for you to get a message to us."

She took a deep breath and looked at the horizontal descent pods. "It's just a shame we can't transmit through that cloud . . . "

Rex raised his hand.

"Yes?"

"So if we get hurt or something, the pod comes back up *without* us?"

Schlott nodded. "Yes."

A murmur rustled through the group.

"And what happens then? To us, I mean, stuck on the ground?" Rex wrung his hands together. Schlott shot Yoné a meaningful glance and looked around, avoiding Rex's eyes.

"Well," she said, her voice softer, "let's just hope that doesn't happen."

THREE

ADAY PASSED BEFORE THE WEATHER changed for the worse.

Although Rex had been working to calm his nerves during the wait, the time in the warehouse protected him and the team from being overcome by cold. At least here he was able to keep busy checking and preparing his gear, as well as getting used to handling the Stær gun. The device seemed simple enough: a handle, a trigger, a safety, a power supply wire that connected to a battery pack on his back, and the muzzle, which, according to Schlott, "you only point at something you want to kill."

"They're really easy," Yoné reassured him. "When you pull the trigger, all it does is thump, and ten little tracer lights fly out of the front. That's it."

"When did *you* shoot one?" Rex asked, slipping the Stær back into its sleek black holster that fastened to the left side of his belt.

"Shhh," she grinned and winked. "It was an accident during a training run last year. I was showing one to some new recruits and shot it over the edge of Island Three. I'm sure the charge was gone when it landed. Otherwise I might've fried a Cthonian!" Yoné stifled a chuckle.

Rex hesitated and looked around.

"Yoné?"

"Yes?"

"Don't you think someone else should be in the group other than me? I told you about this before. I'm only sixteen, and I was *just* put into the ACF with no training. Something's happening that . . . "

"Shh!" Yoné cut him off. She looked around,

fearful they'd been overheard. She covered her Tracker with her hand to keep it from detecting her words, leaned in close to Rex's ear, and whispered, "Cover *that*." She nodded toward his Tracker. He placed his hand over the device and squeezed. "And *I* told you: There are things going on you don't know about. You are different, and it's supposed to be this way. Powerful people want you here. And there's nothing I can do but try and keep you safe. I wish I could; I really do. But I can do nothing— nothing but follow orders. There are no missteps in Ætheria. You of all people should know that by now." She leaned out and adopted a more confident posture. She released her Tracker. Rex did the same. She spoke in a louder voice, clearly wanting others to hear.

"So just remember to aim high, since the charges typically drop in the air—especially if you shoot from far away." She widened her eyes as she looked at Rex, indicating he needed to answer in an equally loud voice. Rex felt that as an actor, Yoné was not doing a good job. She was a much better Point.

"I'll remember it," Rex said, trying to force confidence. But despite the tone in his voice, anger and fear churned within. He felt trapped, imprisoned, watched. And now, he felt in danger. Who could possibly care if he was or wasn't part of the ACF? His mother was gone. His foster father was dead. It didn't make sense.

With his pack ready, his uniform checked and double-checked, and his vitals sensors stuck to his chest and connected via three small wires to his pack, all Rex had left to do was to make sure that his SCRM—his Self-Contained Respirator Mask—was stocked with oxygen and that none of its hoses or rubber seals were cracked. The last thing he wanted to do was make it through the stormy Welcans cloud only to suffocate once his feet hit the ground. For everyone knew that the surface of Cthonia was inhospitable. When he was younger, Rex had even heard rumors that you could only survive two minutes down there without supplemental oxygen, and that the terror and pain of not being able to take a breath were indescribable. But it had never occurred to him to ask how anyone knew this. Now that they knew the Cthonians were still around, part of him wondered if the Cthonian society might not also be divided between the haves and the have-nots: just like in Ætheria, those who are allowed masks and those who just have to adapt to a dangerous—and potentially deadly—environment . . .

"Unit Alif, prepare for dispatch!" Schlott's command jerked Rex from what felt like his thousandth review of his gear. He jumped and looked up. Schlott had decided they would go down in the same groups as before, since, according to her, "you're already working as a team."

Rex's heart thumped in his throat. His hands became moist. He stepped up to his descent pod: Pod Two. He would descend right after Yoné, who would go first. He glanced at the others. Everyone seemed eaten with the same anxiety. But right now, he couldn't afford to be distracted. Right now all that mattered was surviving the descent and then surviving whatever lay below.

As his pod opened, Rex looked in at a vast array of screens, blinking lights, and a padded, body-length seat with four separate straps to keep him in. He peered at the screens and noticed that there was one for altitude, one for outside conditions, and one for vital statistics. His eyes fell on the blue emergency return button.

His thoughts swirled back to his first descent into the Proboscis three days ago: then he'd climbed down; then he'd been terrified of the racking, creaking, and popping static electricity that had made their descent almost impossible; then he'd gotten a glimpse of the body and of some sort of Cthonian encampment below, but he'd never imagined himself now part of a team heading all the way down . . . and out.

"Take your places!" Schlott shouted. Rex noticed

that the tone in her voice was not angry or domineering, but concerned. It was a new tone. Did she harbor the same worry as Rex and the others? Did she have family on Ætheria she was worried about? Did she lose any loved ones in the attack?

As Rex stepped into the pod and lay back into the padded seat, he decided she must've lost someone. How could anyone closely connected with the Ætherian Council not have? It was only natural that they would've been working in the Power Works. Even if she hadn't lost someone directly in the attack, then surely she was worried about what would happen to her loved ones if the ACF couldn't repair the Proboscis quickly. They would all die.

Rex reached down and strapped himself in. With each click of the metal belt buckles, his heart lurched. He glanced down and noticed an oxygen container strapped to the inside left side of the pod. He then laid his head back into the headrest and tried to calm his breathing. He looked straight up, his view framed by the sides of the pod, which felt more and more like a coffin. He allowed his eyes to scan the warehouse's ceiling, which was little more than a crisscross of interconnected triangles, forming a geodesic dome.

By his sides, his hands began to rap the sides of the pod and his pants. He was shaking. He clenched his fists and scrunched up his face, fighting off his fear. Memories of his first claustrophobic experience with the SCRM mask came flooding back. Then, he'd fainted. He was far more terrified now than before. He wasn't just wedging his head and face into a rubber mask; he was placing his entire body into a container that would be held over a thirty thousand foot drop by only a thin, metal wire.

Several yards away, the *clump-clump* of footsteps made their way closer. Step, step, pause, mumble, mumble, *cla-clunk*! Schlott was moving from pod to pod, saying something to each scout, and closing and locking the hatches.

Breathe, breathe, relax . . .

Schlott's head appeared within the black frame

of the pod, blocking out the geometric ceiling and causing Rex to jump. The restraints dug into his legs and torso, where he'd tightened them . . . a bit too much, he now realized.

"Okay, Rex, it's time. You'll need to go ahead and put on your SCRM mask and give me the thumbs-up that you're breathing fine. And I need to hook up these." She leaned in and took the rubber supply tube from Rex's mask and screwed it onto the oxygen tank. She turned the nozzle, and the tank let out a hiss as air flowed from the canister and into the mask. Schlott then pulled some wires from beside one of the screens and clamped a glowing red sensor onto Rex's right index finger.

"You have your backpack, which is monitoring you. When you get down below, you will need to switch from the pod's oxygen to the one in your pack. That way you can move around down there without suffocating. Here," she pointed to a red screen in front of him, "this will let you keep track of your vitals as you go down." She tapped the screen, which was just to the right of the altimeter screen. Rex tried to follow her pointing, but found himself focusing on the soft blue numbers: 35,121 feet. But when the sensor picked up a signal from his finger, the smaller screen blinked to life, flashing several statistics in red:

```
HR 123/min

O2 Sat 88%

BP 120/65
```

Schlott glanced at the screen.

"One hundred and twenty-three beats per minute?" She faced Rex. "Just calm down. Big breaths. You'll be fine. You'll see. But breathe through this." She pulled his SCRM up from its clip on his chest harness and worked it around his head. As the rubber mask covered his face, the clear eye goggles fogged with his rapid exhales. Schlott pulled the mask back over his head, the rubber sticking to Rex's hair and pulling it painfully across his scalp. All sounds became muffled under the rubber—all except that of Rex's own breathing, which now seemed amplified and mechanic. Still, with each inhale, Rex felt stronger and stronger, and his thoughts became clearer and clearer. Breathing the purer oxygen was like a drug; Rex wanted to hog a canister for himself and do nothing but breathe as much in as possible and as quickly as possible. More than this, he never wanted to give the oxygen up, now that he was tasting the full life it could give.

"Look," mumbled Schlott, tapping on Rex's shoulder to make sure he was listening. He made eye contact with her through the now dissipating condensation on the inside of the eye lenses. He nodded that he heard her.

"These vitals are for *you* to keep track of yourself, not us. Because once you enter the Welcans cloud, the fermionic lithium will block all transmissions. If something happens to you in the cloud, there's not a lot we can do. And it's mainly for you to monitor your O2 saturation level, here." She pointed to the screen. "If it drops below eighty percent, you press the blue button," she pointed, "and you'll come back up. But *don't* press it unless you have to, because it will force everyone behind you to come back up as well. Do you understand?"

"Yes," Rex said. The booming sound of his own voice in his SCRM mask made his ears ring. Images of his mother's face danced across his starry gaze. Did she still look like the image in the photograph? Or had she visibly aged? Was she even still alive?

"Good! Remember: Get to the ground and head to the destruction site. Don't wait for the others to follow. Be careful, get intel, and help us!"

Rex closed his eyes and nodded. In one smooth movement, Schlott patted him on the shoulder and stood, disappearing from the black frame. In the next breath, the pod's hatch closed. From outside, the latches were snapped into place with metallic clunks, and Rex was bathed in darkness, the only light teasing him from the screens and controls just a foot from his face.

When Rex had put his SCRM mask on for the

first time two weeks ago, his mind had quickly spun into a whirlwind of panic. He had been able to muster the courage to continue on his Auscultor mission by thinking of his mother, whose blurry face hovered in front of him like some far-off dream. Now, doubly closed inside the rubbery SCRM mask and this high-tech coffin, Rex felt the familiar pangs of terror welling up once more. A cold sensation—a burning chill—inched out from his chest and into his limbs. His face went frigid as his heartbeat quickened. His eyes went in and out of focus, but the blinking red heart rate monitor stirred him from his torpor:

HR 130

HR 142

HR 170

"Stop it!" he shouted to himself. He felt the inside of the rubber mask go wet from the outburst of hot, humid air. He shook his head and pounded his fists into the black cushioned seat, which was now hidden in his dark enclosure.

Rex closed his eyes. He would ignore the flashing red light, no matter what it told him. He wouldn't look again, no matter what.

In the dance of stars, swirls, and fireworks that popped against the backdrop of his closed eyelids, Rex noticed another face that was shifting in and out of focus. It wasn't his mother this time. It was Yoné. And then Deputy Head Schlott. And then both faces blended into one. Both of them as one seemed to be peering at him through the dark. With his eyes closed, he tried to focus on their unified and combined features, but he found that all he could discern was the vague silhouette of these two women who had come into his life, and all because of two tragedies heaped on top of each other: his forced recruitment and the attack on Tátea's Power Works.

"It'll be alright, Rex," they seemed to say with one voice. "It'll be alright. I'll be with you . . . I'll be with you . . . " Rex felt his breathing slow and a new calm work through his limbs. He took a deep breath—deep enough to fill his entire torso from the belly up with air, so much so that he felt a relaxing stretch from the inside of his ribcage.

Thwonk!

The pod lurched to the side with a crash. It rumbled and shook. Someone outside was rolling it across some sort of track, whose metallic rails Rex could hear through the bottom of the enclosure. He recalled seeing the network of rails when he'd entered the warehouse. Now he knew what they were for. He was being moved into position.

Ka-clunk!

The pod was lifted and positioned at a slight angle. Rex felt his body wanting to slide in the direction of his feet, but the four straps held him in place.

He opened his eyes.

I can do this.

Even though no one could see him, Rex nodded, as if to convince himself. He took another deep breath, but this time smiled when the vapor from his exhale clouded his eye lenses.

The pod lurched forward, slid along an inclined rail, and seemed to hang for a moment, as if suspended in midair. Rex understood that he was hovering over the trapdoor he'd seen earlier.

Another *clunk*, another lurch, and the pod rotated steeply down. With a jerk, it began its long descent down the guy wire and toward the Welcans cloud—toward Cthonia.

FOUR

ACCORDING TO SCHLOTT, ALL REX AND THE others had to do was "relax" as their pods made their way to Cthonia's surface, which was meant to take about thirty minutes. Unlike when he climbed down the Proboscis, this was less demanding. Then, Rex had had a wider and longer field of vision. And at least then he'd had the sense of having some control over how and at what speed he descended. But now he was powerless—exposed to whatever might happen to him from the outside. The storm? Lightning? Cthonians firing from below? Descent pod failure? Yes, they were heading down five miles away from the attack site and in a pouring gale of acidic rain, but also no one knew what awaited them on the other side of the Welcans cloud.

Rex let his gaze fall on the emergency rise button. Not that he wanted to press it, but more to reassure himself that at least he had some say in his fate, if he needed it.

The pod rattled and wiggled as it descended. He couldn't see out, but Rex could tell from the altimeter that his descent was steady:

```
28,837 feet
27,675 feet
25,523 feet
```

Soon watching the numbers decrease became a type of meditation, and this allowed him to stave off waves of claustrophobia that reared their heads.

When he'd gone down before, he'd worn an earpiece in his SCRM mask, which had let him communicate with Yoné and the others in his group. But now, all he had were the creaks and rattles of this nightmare ride—that, and his pounding heartbeat.

25,100 feet

23,034 feet

20,945 feet

As he neared twenty thousand feet, Rex heard the beginnings of a new sound: not a creak or rattle, but a rumble. Low and guttural at first, the rumble grew, and was soon broken by a bone-cracking *Boom!* that made the pod shake. The jolt caused Rex's breath to falter and his heartbeat to spike again to over one-forty.

Thunder. He was entering the Welcans cloud and the storm.

Keeping his eyes riveted on the altimeter, Rex tried to time his breath with the descending feet.

Boom! Boom-Boom!

With each crash, the number of feet per breath decreased, though the rate of descent stayed the same. At first the thunder had been farther off to the right or left—it was difficult to tell. Soon Rex felt as though every explosion would rattle the pod to bits and either kill him with one final jolt of a billion volts or crack his pod open like a pistachio, sending his body hurtling through space to the ground below. He could feel his hands trembling, soaked with sweat. He began muttering to himself. He was not reciting any sort of prayer. His mouth was unconsciously forming vowels and consonants. It was as if his fear had taken a life of its own.

Boom!

With the most violent thunderclap yet, the pod shook as if rattled about by an unseen giant's hand. The dials and screens flickered, and crackles of static electricity popped around Rex's body, making his extremities tingle. Even though the altimeter maintained its steady descent, Rex closed his eyes and continued mumbling. He was covered in sweat and racked with chills. The entire pod shook in frequency with the guy wire, whose miles-long expanse shuddered in the wind outside. Until this point, Rex's mind had been clear of his earlier fears. Now he could not rid himself of the repeating image of the silver clasps losing their grip on the guy wire in the rain and slipping, sending the pod sliding down the remaining nineteen thousand feet. From a drop of that height, he would surely land at a speed of nearly four hundred miles per hour, instantly crushing him, the pod, and Yoné's pod below. *If that happens*, he thought, *I only hope she'll be out of her own pod and clear of the impact.*

17,238 feet

Rex didn't know how long he'd been tossed about and thunderbolted in the Welcans cloud. There were no clocks among his dials. Perhaps he'd been in the storm for two minutes, perhaps ten.

But just when the terror of sliding down the guy wire to his death was becoming suffocating and unbearable, the pod stopped shaking. It still rattled, but the rattle was more of a calm vibration than a tremor. The din of the thunder and the storm outside ceased. Rex tried to steady his breath and listen—through his SCRM mask and through the insulated sides of the pod. He thought he could hear a steady stream of water tapping on the outside. *Was that rain?*

And then he realized: he'd made it through the Welcans cloud and was now *below*, in the Cthonian realm of weather. He was entering *their* world—the other world, the world talked about in stories and rumors that he'd heard since he was a kid. A world he'd wondered even more about ever since seeing those three bodies in the morgue. And a world he'd only glimpsed through the gash in the side of the Proboscis.

He wondered about the people who lived in Cthonia, about their massive size and pale features. He wondered what sort of language they spoke and how they lived their lives. He wondered what sort of stories and rumors they told each other about Ætheria . . . especially now that they were sending spies up. Above all, he wondered what it would be like to stand face-to-face with a breathing, living Cthonian. Would they be enemies from the start, or would they have anything in common? How human *were* they?

Brrrrrrrrrrrr . . .

The pod buzzed and hummed as it descended. Every now and then, Rex heard a high-pitched *twang!* as the guy wire outside stretched and flexed under the weight of what now must've been the ten pods. *How strong are these wires?* he wondered. Not only were they supporting the weight of the descending team, but the pull of Island Twenty-Three up above must've been massive as well. He couldn't remember ever hearing of one of the support guy wires snapping on their own, but there was a first time for everything. Until now, the only part of Ætheria he'd ever seen falter or fall was Tátea's Power Works . . .

5,934 feet

5,300 feet

4,969 feet

HR 84

HR 95

HR 111

Rex's breathing came faster and faster. He was now less than a mile above Cthonia's surface and far closer than he'd been before when the team went down the Proboscis. Then, they'd only barely gone below the Welcans cloud and were still about three or four miles up.

He wanted to call out to Yoné, just to hear her voice, but he had no radio connection. *Stupid*, he thought. Sure, radio signals couldn't go through the Welcans cloud, but what about now, now that they were completely clear of the cloud? *Why didn't the Ætherian engineers who designed these things think about the need to communicate down here? Who made these decisions? No radio seems to add unnecessary danger to the whole mission.*

HR 138

Bam!

The pod jerked to a stop. The purring and buzzing ceased. The only sound now was the rain outside and Rex's heart. In the distance, Rex could make out thunder that still rumbled up above in the Welcans cloud. He looked at the altimeter.

485 feet

What? There must've been a problem. Why was he stuck this high up? What was happening?

HR 132

O2 98%

At least his SCRM mask was working.

Boom!

Something rapped into his pod from above. It must've been the rest of the team, whose pods were settling in place on top of his. Rex imagined the scene from the outside. From a mile away, he imagined that it looked like a giant bead necklace.

He waited. He listened. He tried to steady his breathing.

Because he didn't have a clock in the pod, he had no idea how long he sat there, waiting and listening to the storm. The only thing he could think was that Yoné's pod had malfunctioned and gotten stuck, causing the backup. They weren't climbing back up, so she couldn't have pressed the emergency button. Had she stopped the pods on purpose?

Knock, knock, knock!

Rex jumped at the sound of someone rapping on his pod's hatch just as if someone were knocking on his door at home. For a second, Rex tried to convince himself he'd only imagined it. But did he? His oxygen saturation was fine, so there was no reason to think that he was hallucinating or hearing things.

Knock, knock, knock!

"Rex!" a muffled voice cried out from outside. He hadn't imagined it. "Open up! We're here!"

What?

Rex stirred in his vertical seat, which was tilted slightly with the angled guy wire. He reached up with his right hand and unfastened his chest harness. As the nylon strap released, he fell forward a few inches and his lungs expanded fully, as if stretching themselves after a long sleep. Until now he hadn't realized how cramped he'd been.

He reached up and tugged gently at his SCRM mask to make sure that the seal was tight. He didn't want his first experience on Cthonia to be suffocation. He leaned down and twisted the mask supply tube from the pod's oxygen tank. With a *hiss* and a *pop*, a small puff of vapor burst from the tube's connecting joint. He lifted the connector to his backpack oxygen supply nozzle and connected the two. Reaching farther back, be fumbled around for the open valve and twisted. A fresh *swoosh* of bottled oxygen again flowed into his mask and over his face, cooling his sweat-covered skin. He once again breathed deeply, as if to check that what he was breathing was actually oxygen. The air felt life-giving and pure, and his thoughts remained crisp. He took another deep breath and eased his hand forward to the hatch release latch. He twisted.

With an ear-popping *swoosh*, swelteringly hot and humid air rushed into the descent pod's compartment. If he had not been fastened in, the sudden gush of air and change in air pressure could easily have swept him out of the pod.

Someone pulled the door open from outside.

Before he could see who it was, Rex found himself scanning this new world. Which, from his point of view, seemed little more than a dimly glowing yellowish cloud with torrents of rain that swirled around and into the pod's compartment, soaking him. It was still night, but dawn was approaching.

Feeling the water, Rex suppressed the urge to laugh. He'd never seen rain before. Nor had he ever felt this kind of warmth before—at least warmth that was natural. Back in Ætheria, all water came from reserves that had been piped up from below, purified, and pumped to the different houses throughout the archipelago. And all the heat was gas-generated. The only weather he'd ever experienced had been intense and frigid winds, along with blinding and unfiltered ultraviolet rays from the sun. Such was life above the clouds in his vertical world.

"Rex, c'mon! Let's go!" the silhouette shouted again, reaching in to unbuckle Rex. It was Yoné. She pointed to a small, latched door just in front of his feet. "In that compartment next to your right knee, there's a wire ladder. Grab it! Let's go!" She then disappeared into the night, leaving Rex alone in the descent pod.

"I got this," Rex said, leaning over to unbuckle his remaining straps. In the rain, his wet, gloved hands slipped over the buckles several times before he could get a good hold. He struggled with an intense urge to lean up and just look outside, amazed at the rain, the warmth, and seeing the Welcans cloud from below, which flashed yellowish-white every few seconds from lightning bursts.

With his straps unbuckled, Rex pulled the rolled wire ladder from the side storage compartment and hooked the top rungs onto the hatch's edge.

It jangled and banged against the descent pod as it unrolled. With his left hand, he reached around to his backpack and worked his headlamp from the side pocket, where he'd packed it earlier. He clamped his hand on the pod's hatch, turned on his headlamp, and looked out.

What he saw stunned him.

Looking down, he saw Yoné's pod standing erect and directly below his. The two were touching. If you didn't know the two were attached to the guy wire stretching up to Ætheria, you'd think the coffin-shaped pods were balanced on top of each other. From the front, the wire was hidden, after all. Below her pod, featureless, wet sand covered the ground. The Cthonian soil was right there: Yoné's pod has stopped because it had hit ground. Then Rex understood. The altimeter reading of four hundred and eighty-five feet must've been feet *above sea level.* It made sense.

He looked up and saw that the sand stretched in all directions. He was in a desert. Seeing this, he remembered the view he'd had from the hole in the Proboscis when the ACF Auscultor unit had found the decomposing Cthonian body: desert and rocks as far as the eye could see, with mountains interrupting only the western horizon. But then he'd been several miles up. Now he was right here.

Rex peered through the dark, trying to see the mountains. But all he saw was rain and the faint glow from intermittent lightning above.

Down below, Yoné had jumped from her pod and was checking her gear belt and Stær gun. Her round, white headlight danced around as she moved. As if sensing Rex's eyes on her, she looked up, her headlamp blinding him.

"What are you waiting for? Come on!" she shouted through her SCRM mask. With the ten feet or so separating them, the layers of rubber in between her mouth and his ears, and the pelting rain all around, he could barely make out her words. And then there was a click in Rex's ears and Yoné's voice became clear, transmitted through their now functioning radio. "Don't cause a backup. We've got work to do!" *That's right*, he thought, *we're below the cloud. The radios work now.*

At that moment, several wire ladders flew past Rex, unrolling as the others threw them down from above. Rex looked up and saw ten more glaring white headlamps working their way down. He swore at himself and tossed his ladder out. It unrolled with a hissing *clankclankclank* and smacked the muddy ground, with nearly fifty more feet still coiled up. Not wanting to be seen less prepared than the others for the assignment, he rotated his body and lowered his foot out until it rested on the top rung. Feeling the ladder clamped in place, he shimmied down the short ten feet to the ground.

Splash.

His feet stuck in a mixture of dirt and rain. He pulled up each foot and could hear a sucking sound. The mud was thick, like glue. His legs trembled from the nervousness and excitement of placing his feet on this strange new world—one that was truly horizontal, and not vertical, like Ætheria. He stepped away from the ladders to give the others space to come down. As they did, he looked around.

Unlike in Ætheria, where the only plant life was contained under geothermic domes to create enough heat and humidity at the high altitudes, here there were no plants—just blackish-brownish rocks, mud, and dried-up sticks and logs scattered around that looked as though they'd been here for centuries. Had there once been a forest here? Plants? The logs would suggest so.

Then Rex remembered what Protector Challies had said about the weather here. The rain was highly acidic—"Enough," he'd said once during the training, "to pickle vegetables. But when we send people down for inspections, their suits, masks, and gloves protect them. The acid wouldn't burn you right away, but it would irritate your skin if you spent several hours in it." That was it. The rain must've killed all the plants and vegetation around. But for how far did the desert unroll? Were there parts of Cthonia that had plants? Rex lifted his hand above his eyes to shield his goggles from the rain. Turning off his headlamp to reduce the glare, he peered out into the darkness, his eyes straining to see anything beyond the wet, messy sludge where they'd landed.

In his immediate vicinity, all he could see was a network of gray guy wires and whitish stratoneum struts—both of which worked together to hold up Island Twenty-Three far above. Rex followed the struts up with his eyes, but they disappeared in the rain and dark. Lowering his gaze, he rotated his head slowly, deliberately scanning the horizon. Behind him, the last of the former Auscultors were planting their feet into the foreign mud. As they did, he could see each hesitate and look around, as if in a daze. They, too, must've been amazed by this new world.

Something caught his eye.

"Yoné!" he shouted, turning around. Hearing her

name, Rex's Point stepped over, holding her head at an angle to avoid blinding him with her headlamp.

"What is it?"

"Look," he said, pointing. "That way. Through the dark. Do you see something?"

"Lemme see." Yoné reached around to the back of her gear belt and unfastened an unseen device, which she raised to her face. Binoculars. She scanned the direction Rex had pointed, her middle finger reaching over the top of the lenses to adjust the focus. She paused.

"That's it," she said, lowering the binoculars and handing them to Rex. "Good work. You found it."

"Found what?" Rex scrunched up his eyebrows under his SCRM mask and pulled the eyepieces to his goggles.

At first, all he could make out through the binoculars was dark, made blurry by the raindrops flowing over the lenses and his goggles. He shifted his head in the direction where he'd spotted the . . .

And then he saw it.

Through the dark, through the rain, several soft orange glows pierced the night. It looked as if small fires were burning in different spots on some massive mound, despite the torrential rain. Rex wondered if the fires hadn't been larger before, and the rain was putting them out. White and black smoke billowed from the constellation of oranges, fading off into the night. The fires seemed miles away.

"What is it?" he asked.

To his right, Yoné *humphed* in disgust.

"You're looking at what's left of Tátea's Power Works."

FIVE

"LIGHTS OFF!" YONÉ SNAPPED, MAKING REX jump and almost drop the binoculars. "Everyone, gather around!"

Before he could follow her order, Rex felt Yoné's hand scrabble up and turn his own headlamp off with a click and a push that was a little too hard. Around him, the other lights clicked off, leaving the team in darkness. As Rex's eyes adjusted, he could barely make out the others' silhouettes. The scouts inched in together, the edges of their shoulders and heads glistening slightly from the rain, which continued to pour. The sky flashed angrily, and up above Rex caught sight of a lightning bolt popping in between the Welcans cloud and one of the stratoneum struts. His breath faltered at the sight. He'd never seen anything so naturally awesome and powerful.

"Can you all hear me?" Yoné shouted through her transmitter. Her voice crackled clearly into Rex's SCRM mask. A chorus of "Yes!" filled his ears. Everyone's radios seemed to be working. "Good," she shouted.

"Yes, I can hear you fine," Rex said.

"Okay," Yoné continued. "I need everyone to look this way."

In the dark, Rex saw Yoné rotate her body and turn to point where the two had just looked through the binoculars. Through the rivulets of rain flowing over his lenses, Rex could barely make out the glints of orange and yellow flickering in the distance. He heard a few of the team members gasp.

"See that?" Yoné said. "That's what's left of Tátea's destroyed Power Works. Even though it fell three days ago, parts of it seem to still be burning. From the looks of it, it also landed on the Cthonians' encampment. Who knows if any survived? And if they did, where might they be?" She shook her head in the dark. "I don't see why they'd hang around, but where would they go? Anyway, we should be just less than five miles away right here. Our job is to work our way over there, but in the dark. We don't know who might be wandering about, and we don't want to give them any reason to find us. Stær guns out!"

With trembling hands, Rex reached down and withdrew his Stær gun, which had been holstered at his left side. He flipped its on switch on the handle of the gun. The device buzzed to life, its power light flickering from red to green. Other green dots appeared around the team's huddle as the other scouts pulled out their guns and turned them on.

"Because of the dark, we'll need to stay within three to five yards of each other," Yoné said. "From what we know, this land is pretty much flat, but what you've got to watch out for are the guy wires and the struts. In the dark, you don't want to get clotheslined! Got it?"

"Got it!" the chorus said.

"Okay, let's head that way, keeping an eye out for *any* movement. Follow my lead. Let's go!"

Without waiting for an answer, Yoné spun on her heels and walked in the direction of the fires. Rex fell in line to her left. As he backed away from her, he kept his eyes on her silhouette, stopping just when her form began to blend in with the darkness around her. He turned his right side to her and walked, his left hand holding the Stær gun at waist level, its muzzle pointed forward.

With each step, Rex had to struggle between his nervousness at their assignment and the wonder of being in this strange new place. Still wearing his AeroGel suit, which had allowed him—and everyone else—to survive the frigid temperatures of Ætheria thirty-five thousand feet above the ground, Rex now found himself sweltering, groaning in a torpid heat he'd never experienced before. His entire body felt soaked on the inside of the suit—not from the rain that was covering him in the first natural, unprocessed water he'd ever encountered, but from sweat—more sweat than he'd produced in his lifetime. Or at least that's the way it felt to him. His armpits felt clammy, he had to blink away stinging drops of perspiration that coursed into his eyes, and his palms slipped inside his gloves. On the outside, his body was overstimulated by the sensation of thousands of drops of acidic water pattering down on his head, his shoulders, his arms, and his back. He had to fight the urge to look up and marvel at the rain—to try and spot its origin in the Welcans cloud, which he could see only in the frequent explosions of lightning that lit up the whole sky and the deserted landscape below. And despite his discomfort, he couldn't remove his suit and expose his skin to the rain. He knew it was acidic, and he knew that any contact would cause irritation.

With each flash of lightning, Rex had a brief image of their layout seared into his retinas: nine other scouts, glistening and drenched from the rain, working their way step-by-step over a vast muddy plain, which, aside from the guy wires and stratoneum struts that pushed up from the ground like prison bars, was flat, desolate, and empty.

How could anyone live down here? Rex wondered, remembering all the times he'd learned in school and from his dad that the atmosphere and conditions on Cthonia rendered all life impossible, and that the only way the Cthonians could breathe was by constant use of respirator masks. It was, after all, because of the ever-more toxic atmosphere down below that Ætheria was founded in the first place all those hundreds of years ago. *But then again,* Rex thought, *if we've managed to create an environment and survive up there, where it's so cold and there's no water, couldn't people have done the same thing down here? Did they really spend their entire lives with respirator masks on? Was that really the only way they could breathe?* As much as Rex hated having his own SCRM mask on for several hours, such an existence seemed unbearable.

After about thirty minutes, Rex noticed his legs were becoming tired—more tired than he'd ever noticed before. *Why?* And then he realized: on the islands of Ætheria, he'd never had to walk this far in one go. Yes, he did sports at school, but that was in one of the geodomes and just running around and playing—not walking nonstop. Even then, he could never run too much, because anything faster than a brisk walk could lead to hypoxia and unconsciousness. Also, with each step on Cthonia, his feet seemed to soak up an extra layer of mud, making them heavier and heavier.

"Ah!" Something whipped up from the dark and struck Rex across the chest, throwing him backwards. He landed on his rear in the mud, his hands out to his sides. His Stær gun tumbled into a puddle to his right, and his heart leapt into his throat. Just as his body came to rest, a flash of lightning shot across the sky. He looked up and glimpsed his attacker.

"What is it?" Yoné snapped through his earpiece. Rex's face burned with embarrassment.

"Nothing," he answered. "I ran into a guy wire. Just call me an idiot, okay?"

"Yeah, well, I told you about those, didn't I?" Yoné's voice burned with sarcasm, but Rex thought he heard her stifle a chuckle.

"Yes, yes. *Thanks.*"

Rex shook his head and reached over for his Stær gun, whose green light shone like a small beacon in the night. He pulled the weapon out of the water and shook it off, inspecting it closely. *Are these things waterproof?* he wondered. *And acid proof?* He doubted it. Why would anyone on Ætheria even think to make them that way?

He stood and glanced around at the others, who were little more than a few faint silhouettes and eleven other green dots. *Still, we came down in the rain, didn't we? Wasn't that the whole point—to wait until we'd be covered by the bad weather so we couldn't be seen? Surely Schlott wouldn't have sent us down with weapons that would fry at the first sign of water . . .* Having convinced himself, Rex stood, scraped the mud off of his rear and his hands, and continued walking. Once again he held his Stær gun ready with his left hand, while he now held out his right hand in front of him, ready for any more guy wires or stratoneum struts.

———

Two hours passed. Because of the dark, the rain, and caution, the team moved at an excruciatingly slow pace. But slowly, surely, the orange flames grew larger, and soon the lightning flashes revealed new obstructions. There, twisted and gnarled among the intact guy wires and the struts, a mangled mess of bent and snapped metal wove its way through the architectural network like evil, mechanical snakes, frozen and waiting. These were parts of the Power Works stratoneum frame that had disintegrated and spread out over a hundred yards during its fall.

As the scouts approached the actual wreckage, the garbled tangle slowed the team even further—with metal lying in a mess around their feet, they now had to dodge that, as well as the chest-high guy wires. The lightning flashes helped them navigate some, but they had to be careful.

When the team got to within fifty yards of the Power Works wreck, the rain abated and Rex could distinguish the remnants of the building where his foster dad had gone to work . . . while he was alive. It was also the factor that had provided water, electricity, and heat for all of Ætheria. The rain came in a slow drizzle, and as the drops thinned, Rex noticed the sky had just begun to glow with the approaching morning.

"Unit Alif, hold back," Yoné's voice sounded through Rex's earpiece. The scouts stopped. At first Yoné said nothing more. Rex glanced to his right and could make out the silhouette of her head scanning the remains of Tátea's Power Works. She seemed to be thinking, trying to make up her mind what to do next. Rex faced forward.

From just looking at the rubble, Rex couldn't imagine that what lay in front of him used to contain Ætheria's most technologically advanced machinery and technology: pumps, filtration systems, generators, computer hubs, oxygen purification manifolds . . . The pile of debris that now smoldered in front of him seemed to be made only of organic material: rocks, dirt, and seeping water. At its highest, the mound was five yards high. From there it tapered off in both directions. At times its contours rose and dipped like a large-scale miniature model of some foreign landscape—but one devastated by fire and torrential rain. Intact, the Power Works building had been nearly forty yards long and twenty yards high. Now it was little more than a devastated splat in the mud. Every inch of the wreckage glistened from the acid rain, and every twenty or thirty feet, flames lapped up from deep below, sending plumes of blackish smoke up to fight against the remaining raindrops.

Aside from the patter of the dwindling rain and the occasional *crack* and *pop* of one of the fires, all was silent. The entire team stood frozen, watching, waiting. But for what? As if afraid that someone might see his movement, Rex swiveled his head slowly, scanning every visible corner of the rubble for signs of life, of movement, of anything other than death. *How many people had been in the Power Works when it went down?* A wave of nausea surged through him: somewhere in all this, his foster dad's body lay crushed. *Or maybe he was still alive?* Rex's thoughts raged: would the Ætherian Council send down a rescue force . . . something other than just ten scouts to see what had happened? *Surely they would,* he thought. *Surely their thoughts are above all on saving their own. And the Cthonians? At the moment, they are nowhere to be seen. How could the Ætherian Council even be sure that it was the*

Cthonians who'd attacked? What if some accident had triggered the explosion? The Proboscis was hundreds of years old, after all. What if it had just been a coincidence that those Cthonians had been coming up the Proboscis right before the . . .

"Team, move in," Yoné said, snapping Rex out of his reverie. He shook his head to chase away his uncontrolled thoughts and glanced at his Stær gun. Its power light still glowed green. *Getting wet must not have hurt it, after all.* He looked up. Only a few drops fell here and there. The rain had almost completely stopped. The faint glint of lightning reflecting off of the Power Works' remains signaled the passing storm. The rising sun added another dim glow to the side of the rubble facing them. Their backs were to the east, and they were facing west. Yoné stepped forward, signaling to the others to follow.

With each step, Rex's nerves drew tighter. His heart pounded, and he felt sweat running down his back, arms, and legs under his AG suit. His armpits were drenched, and his masked face dripped constantly. With each bead of sweat, he shook his head and blinked to keep the stinging, salty liquid from his eyes. He longed to get out of his suit. Maybe they'd be able to soon, now that the acid rain had stopped? He clutched his Stær gun, keeping it pointed straight ahead. With every third step, he had to shift his gaze from forward to downward as he navigated the twisted wreckage that lay about, making their advance like crossing a minefield.

"Those on the left, look left; those on the right, right. Let's get to the middle and then work our way around."

Rex looked up.

"We're not going to climb over it, are we?" he asked through his mouthpiece.

"No. Too risky. I don't want any of us to fall and break a leg . . . or get burned."

With the wreckage within yards, Rex noticed a new smell working its way through his SCRM mask. It was hard to place, but whatever it was, it smelled rotten, burned—like something had been incinerated and the exhaust was being pumped into his respirator unit. He coughed as a pungent taste filled his mouth. He wanted to spit but couldn't. Instead, he swallowed hard and tried to breathe naturally. He was breathing in the fumes of the smoldering island. A few faint coughs echoed around him. The others were feeling the same thing.

By the time the team reached the edge of the debris, the rain had stopped and the hidden sun was just coming up. If anything, this made listening for other sounds seem easier, but the clear weather and the rising sun made the scouts visible as they advanced. So far, they'd seen no signs of anything other than burning destruction. The entire place felt empty of human life. Rex wondered about the tent complex he'd seen from above while in the Proboscis. He wondered if anyone had been inside when Tátea's Power Works had fallen. Like Yoné, he wondered if there were any Cthonian bodies buried in the rubble—mingled in with the Ætherian bodies. Because from just looking at the now-lit debris, he realized that the Ætherian building had fallen directly on top of the Cthonian encampment.

Yoné pointed to the left. The team followed her lead and turned, beginning a clockwise sweep around the pile of debris, which seemed diamond-shaped. Rex walked with Yoné behind him. Four other scouts spanned out in front.

"We can spread out more, now that we can see," Yoné's voice crackled.

"What if there are . . . Cthonians out here?" Rex asked. "What if they can see us?"

Yoné paused and looked around at the rubble. Rex thought he saw her shrug her shoulders.

"Unlikely," she said. "This place is just a mess—devastation, and that's it. All we need to do is walk around it and see what we can see. Then we'll head back up." She paused, before adding, "Seems to me that if anyone were going to be here—any Cthonians, I mean—we'd have already seen them. Unless they're hiding, but I don't think so . . . "

She kept walking, indicating that the group should do the same.

Up ahead, whoever was on point walked a little faster, which put space between them. Rex squinted through his foggy lenses. Who was that? He couldn't tell, and when they'd lined up earlier at the pods, he hadn't paid attention to who stood where.

As they walked, Rex struggled to keep his eyes forward. He fought a powerful urge to examine the rubble, to see if he could see any signs of life—of someone, anyone, they might save. This urge was mixed with dread that was just as powerful—dread that he might see what he feared the most: his foster dad, dead. While Franklin Strapp had been alive, the two had never been close. But now that he was dead, Rex felt a massive hole open up in his heart. First his mom, then his foster father—the only family he'd ever known. Both of them, gone. And now he was by himself . . .

Every few steps, he glanced at the pile. But with each glance all he saw was crushed metal, pipes, wires, synthetic walls, a dying flame here and there, and thin columns of smoke wafting upward.

He pushed forward, struggling to keep his eyes on the scouts up ahead. They walked in formation, no one saying a word. Rex didn't look eastward, but the sun must've been up by now. All around, a pale yellow glow chased away the shadows of the night. He could clearly see the tapering pile of debris as the team neared what must've been the southernmost tip of the wreckage. Here, the pipes and twisted metal thinned and spread out to form a thin layer of rubble, as opposed to a towering mountain, which broke off suddenly. Before long, the remains of Tátea's Power Works were little more than a scattering of pulverized materials thin enough for the team to turn right and walk straight through.

For the first time since they had landed, Rex looked right, where he could see what lay beyond the devastation.

He saw someone moving.

SIX

"**Y**OU THERE! STOP!"

Before his brain could process what was happening, Rex had shouted into his SCRM mask, causing his ears to ring from the deafening noise of his own voice. Adrenaline shot through his body and his limbs tingled with fight-or-flight energy.

Up ahead, the four scout members were jolted alert, their bodies springing up as if dazed by a Stær gun. They jerked their heads to the right, following Rex's frantic pointing.

"There! There! There!" Rex screamed, turning his body to face what he had seen.

About thirty yards away, a human form was bent over the rubble, rummaging around for something. At first glance, it seemed as if the form were looking for something lost or buried in the Power Works' collapse. But at the sound of Rex's shouts, the form stretched to its full height and faced the team.

From this close distance, Rex saw it was a girl. Her chestnut hair hung down in a tattered mess over her shoulders, and her face was wrought with worry or fear—Rex couldn't tell, because her nose and mouth were covered with some sort of mask. A respirator, no doubt. But he hardly had time to process any of this before he realized that her skin was much paler than any he'd ever seen—except for the Cthonian spies' corpses he'd seen in the morgue back in Ætheria. That, and she was unnaturally tall. Standing at least an entire head over him and the others on his team of scouts, the girl could've been standing right next to Rex and she would've easily seen over his head.

Rex's blood went cold.

He was looking at a living Cthonian.

"Stop! You! Come over here!" Yoné's voice broke the standstill. Rex jerked his head to the right to see his Point jumping over heaps of rock and debris, heading toward the Cthonian girl. Seeing Yoné rush forward, Rex and the others broke into a run that was more of a dance to avoid tripping over the mess covering the ground.

"Stop!" Yoné screamed.

The girl didn't stop. She turned and ran.

With terror flooding his body, Rex lifted his Stær gun and ran alongside his teammates. His panicked breath echoed in his SCRM mask, which filled with vapor, causing him to see things as if through a cloud. Tinges of his previous claustrophobic terror tickled his mind, threatening to paralyze him as he gave chase. But with each surge of fear, he pushed harder from the ground and gripped his weapon with even more determination. He would not let Yoné see him falter again, as he had when he'd first tried on the SCRM mask in Ætheria. Then, he'd passed out. But now, he ran forward.

Up ahead, the girl dashed away, her long legs arching over the rubble like those of a giant yet nimble spider. She moved her spindly arms like an athlete, pumping with each step to run or jump. Whenever she hopped over an obstacle, she seemed to hurl herself into the air. Rex had never seen someone so large, so graceful, or so strong. He imagined that with her strength alone, the girl would be able to fight them all off—if they hadn't been armed.

The chase intensified. With each step, she seemed to put more and more distance between her and the team. She rounded a corner of the mountain of rubble and exploded into a full sprint across a flat expanse. As the landscape opened up, Rex noticed that on this western side of the Power Works' remains, some other substance was mixed in with the rubble. It looked like massive sheets of some kind of white cloth—perhaps tecton, vinyl, or something similar to that used in the Ætherians' AeroGel suits. It almost looked like some sort of temporary structure that might have been in place prior to the attack. This was it: Rex was seeing the remains of the tent he'd seen before, when he and the scouts had gone down the Proboscis—the one that had been connected to the massive tube via a tent-like tunnel. Yoné had been right: the Power Works must've destroyed it as the building fell.

About fifty yards beyond the last pieces of fabric, the landscape was interrupted by the hulking mass of some kind of transportation device. The machine was colossal. It consisted of a metallic round body attached to two flat surfaces extending from the side. On each of the flat wings, two mammoth engines clung like giant parasites hitching a ride. This was some sort of human transport device, and the girl was heading straight for it. Rex was then doubly stunned to see a group of strange animals milling around the machine. Walking on four legs, the animals were covered with thin, brown or black hair. Their bodies seemed powerful, and their tails, long and flowing. Their triangular heads sat atop thick, massive necks, which put their height at more than seven feet. On each of their backs, what appeared to be leather seats were strapped firmly to the animals' bodies. Their feet ended in smooth hooves.

"Stop her!" Yoné shouted. "Fire!" At the sound of Yoné's voice, the animals turned in their direction and ogled the team with frightened eyes.

With trembling hands, Rex lifted his Stær gun to eye level and aimed it at the girl's sprinting, gangly figure. With his mind spinning in a combination of fear, claustrophobia, and nervous terror, he was unable to remember what he'd been told about the gun's range. *Would the charges even reach her from this distance—nearly fifty yards?* Rex didn't have time to wonder. Gripping the gun in his left hand, he balanced the girl's form over the white-dotted sights and pulled the trigger.

Click. Bzzzzzzzzz. Click.

Nothing happened. No charge. No detonation. No firing.

Rex squeezed again and again.

Click. Click. Click.

With mounting horror, he lowered his eyes to look at his weapon, but didn't stop running. The green light still glowed, but the gun was malfunctioning.

The mud, he thought.

"Aaaaahh!" he shouted as something struck his right shin. In his focus on his Stær gun he hadn't watched where he was going, even though he'd maintained his sprint. Whatever had struck him yanked his right leg from under him. And in his momentum, his body hurled forward. Before he could process what was happening, he let go of the gun and pulled out his arms to stop his fall. Something else hit him on the side of the head as he fell. One of the twisted pieces of the Power Works' framework. Its rock-hard yet ultralight stratoneum surface rapped his temple with the force of a cudgel. He saw a flash with the impact, and in a brief second, his field of vision swirled and jerked out of focus. As his body fell forward, his head was pulled back. A strap of his SCRM mask had gotten caught on the metal.

Snap!

With a violent yank, his head popped free and he landed chest-first in the mud.

Like an animal carcass, his rubber respirator mask hung limp on the twisted metal. Rex's face and head were exposed to Cthonia's toxic atmosphere.

In a surge of panic, Rex spun onto his back and threw his hands over his face, holding his breath. His heart pounded against his ribs, his eyes bulged with terror, he was covered with sweat, and his lungs screamed for air. Off to his left, Yoné and one of the other scouts bounded toward Rex, their arms outstretched to help. He couldn't tell where the others were. His vision was going blurry, and his mind swirled with images from the past few weeks as he anticipated the final sting in his throat and lungs that would cause him to pass out and never wake up.

With tears in his eyes, he fumbled into a sitting position and stretched out his left hand for his mask, all the while holding his right inside-elbow tight over his nose and face. His trembling fingers brushed the edge of the rubber mask, but it remained stuck fast on the framework. As it snapped back into place, Rex realized that the hose dangling from the mask had been torn. Even if he had succeeded on putting the SCRM mask on, its connection to oxygen had been cut.

He tried to stand, but his vision darkened. His head spun. Fists grabbed at his shoulders—it must've been Yoné and the others. They seemed to be holding him up. His chest was bursting. Tears streamed down his face. He felt as though a massive person were behind him, squeezing his thorax in a crushing grip. He felt faint. His legs failed him. He began to fall.

And then he released his mouth. His lungs, as if acting of their own accord, inflated.

No sooner had he gulped in Cthonia's foul air than his vision, his mental clarity, and his life returned to him instantly, as if restored by magic. He breathed in again, and the cool, clean oxygen seemed to fill every vein, every capillary, every cell of his body. Not only did his life return to him, but with each breath he felt stronger, more alert, more alive than he'd ever felt before. His vision not only cleared, it became sharp and crisp. His hearing homed in on the slightest noises from miles away. He could even sense Yoné's and the other scouts' body heat as they stood near him. These few breaths made him feel powerful, almost super-human. The sensation reminded him of the euphoria he'd felt when he'd breathed the bottled oxygen. Only now, the sensation was magnified tenfold. He was swimming in an ecstasy of pure, dense air—Cthonian air.

He stood tall and shook off Yoné's hands. Still in her mask, she stepped back and glanced over at the other three scouts who stood near Rex and whom he now saw with clarity. From within her SCRM mask, Yoné's stunned words echoed out.

"Rex . . ."

Rex glanced at her, focusing on her gray eyes through her foggy lenses. He breathed in again and laughed in spite of himself. With every breath he felt stronger—to the point that the desire flashed through him to turn around and root through the rubble with his bare hands to find his foster father.

He looked down at his mask, which hung lifeless on the twisted metal.

He breathed in again and again, as if testing to make sure he wasn't dreaming. Thoughts bombarded him about the meaning of what was happening.

"I can breathe," he finally said, looking at the

others. His voice rang clearer than it ever had. Its effortless volume surprised him and the others, who gave a start. "What's happening? I can't believe it." To show he wasn't exaggerating, he took a few more deep breaths and felt a euphoria unlike anything he'd ever felt before. It felt like a drug—only not one that you ingest or inject, but one that surrounds you and comforts you . . . one that is natural, part of life itself, no, the very *cause* of life. He also realized in that instant that his entire life on Ætheria had been defined by life *without* oxygen—or at least with very little. It was an environment in which you constantly felt sluggish, and in which any effort more than a slow walk would cause dizziness. But not here. Not on Cthonia.

"Trust me," Rex said, laughing like a small child on a sugar high. "It's unbelievable. And it's all fake—*everything* they've told us up there about the air here." He tilted his head upward toward the Welcans cloud, which continued to boil above them. "I can breathe better here than in Ætheria. Try it! Come on!" He giggled childishly as he spoke.

Rex reached out and grabbed Yoné's mask. She swatted his hand away and stepped back. The others made as if to raise their Stær guns, but lowered them. They seemed unsure what to make of what was happening. They too had always been trained and taught to understand that nothing was more toxic than Cthonia's atmosphere. This was, after all, the reason that led to the construction of Ætheria nearly a millennium ago. Ætheria's ancestors had built the stratospheric complex precisely because the air down here was no longer safe. And here was their youngest recruit—who'd been brought into the Ætherian Cover Force because he was "special"—bouncing around and laughing with his mask off. Was he mocking them? Was he crazy? Whatever was happening, one thing was certain: he wasn't dropping dead, which was what they'd always been told would happen if you breathed in Cthonia's air. Almost instant death.

"Rex!" Yoné snapped, stepping back toward him and holding out her hand. "This is insane! How can you be so sure? We've got to get you up, now! You're gonna die if we don't!" To emphasize her point, she pointed off in the direction of the pods, now about five miles away.

"We've . . . the Cthonian . . . but . . . " she mumbled. She fumbled with her Stær gun and fidgeted in place, unsure what to do or what to make of the situation. She was probably realizing that even if they tried to get Rex back to the pods now, they'd have to walk for nearly an hour. She glanced at his disabled SCRM mask and shook her head. The oxygen supply tube was shredded, and no one on the team had the means to repair it. She continued to mumble into her mask, dumbstruck. She was at a loss for words as she began to accept the truth that Rex was not in any danger. And more than that—everything the Ætherian Council had ever told her and the rest of Ætheria about Cthonia was a lie.

"No!" Rex retorted. He reached down and picked up his Stær gun, which he'd dropped. He slid in into his holster and looked around. "I'm telling you, try it! And this air . . . there's something about it . . . I feel stronger than I've ever felt. It's doing something to me. It's like there's even more breathable air here than back home. It's like . . ."

A sucking sound behind him made him jump and whirl around. Ten feet away, one of the other scouts had removed her mask and stood, eyes and mouth agape like a fish out of water, staring at Rex and . . . breathing. As she did, her face gained more color and she too seemed to fill with energy. The euphoria that Rex had just discovered seeped into her pores through her lungs, which had never before breathed such clean air.

Rex stared at her and smiled.

"He's right," the scout said, looking back at Yoné. She too began to laugh. "Try it."

"But . . . but what if it affects you after a while?" blabbered Yoné. "Like some gases. Like carbon monoxide. You can't smell it or anything, and then . . . "

"You fall asleep and die," Rex interrupted her. "I know. But right now, each breath makes me feel better, not worse. No, I'm telling you, I don't know where they got their information up there, whether they misunderstood something, or whether they . . . " His voice trailed off.

"Yoné!" a boy shouted from off behind the group. His voice was muted by a layer of rubber— the SCRM mask. Rex and the others turned toward the voice.

About twenty yards away, the remaining scouts walked toward Rex and the others. Their Stær guns were drawn, but the scouts carried the weapons at their sides. They walked as a small semicircle, the opening of which was facing Rex and the group.

At the center of the semicircle, the Cthonian girl walked, her eyes indignant but worn, a partial respirator mask covering her mouth and nose. As she approached, she kept her eyes riveted on Rex.

The team had captured her.

SEVEN

SCHLOOP. *SCHLOOP, SCHLOOP, SCHLOOP.*

One by one, the scouts pulled off their masks as the Cthonian girl was led up to Yoné. It was as if seeing Rex and the one scout breathing freely triggered something in the team members' minds, and without seeking approval from Yoné or talking with each other, they followed Rex's lead. And in each case, they visibly struggled between the duty to keep a close watch on their prisoner and the exhilaration of the life- and power-giving air that saturated their lungs and bodies. As each glanced around in wonder, color and a never-before-felt vigor flooded their complexions.

"Who are you?" Yoné asked the Cthonian, who kept her eyes on the ground. Rex wondered if the Cthonian was ashamed of something. She seemed to be avoiding looking at any of the scouts.

Rex shifted his gaze back and forth between Yoné and the prisoner. Very little of his previous nervousness was left in his body. The cleansing oxygen seemed to have purified him of any hostile thoughts. *Still,* he reminded himself, *I'm on a mission. Stay focused, stay focused.* He couldn't let himself forget that for whatever reason, this girl probably had a role in the attack on Ætheria. *She* had been involved in the extermination of the Ætherians. *She* had attacked their sole means of staying alive: the power, water, and cthoneum gas purification plant. *She* had wanted them dead. *She* had killed Rex's foster father. And he couldn't let that go, no matter how thrilling the discovery of this new, breathable world proved at that moment.

"Who *are* you?" Yoné repeated, yanking Rex from his thoughts. Yoné stepped up to within a yard of the Cthonian, who towered a good head over Rex's Point. As she stepped up, the Cthonian raised her eyes and looked at Yoné; but she still avoided looking at anyone else. Yoné and the girl sized each other up.

"Well? What's your name? Why are you here? Are there any more of you? Answer me!"

At Yoné's insistent questions, the prisoner remained mute, her stony gaze directed down onto Rex's Point. Rex had the impression of two powerful statues set up opposite each other at the entrance of some important gate. But one was a foot taller than the other.

"She's a little hard to understand," one of the scouts said. "She shouted a few words when we caught up with her, but we only understood a few. Maybe it's because of her mask, too, but she has a weird accent."

"Did you have to daze her?" Yoné asked.

"No. Before we got in range, she surrendered. Said something about help or attack or something. She's been cooperative."

Yoné looked up at the Cthonian, the glare in her eyes softened by this news.

"Do you understand me?"

The prisoner nodded and shook her head. Was this a yes? A no? Something in between?

"What's your name?" Yoné asked again.

To the group's astonishment, the Cthonian reached up and removed her mask. She took a few deep breaths and let the device fall to the ground. Just then Rex realized that, unlike the Ætherians' SCRM masks, hers was not attached to any air supply. It looked more like a particulate mask—the kind you'd wear to keep from breathing in dust or smoke. *But why had she been wearing it?* Rex thought. *Was there some other reason?*

"Aral," the Cthonian answered, her voice much more powerful than Yoné's. It wasn't a shout, but there was something clear, pure about her voice—something that made it carry much more directly through the air. It was almost singsong, while also being commanding. Hearing her speak reminded Rex of the difference in Ætheria between the voices of people with oxygen and without. Those with supplemental air always had stronger voices, whereas those without were more raspy. In just the few minutes he'd been breathing the Cthonian air, Rex's voice had already changed remarkably—it was clear and powerful, so much so that he felt he could shout for miles.

In features, Aral was clearly human, just taller, paler, and more muscular than anyone Rex had known in Ætheria. Rex thought back to the frozen Cthonian spies his dad's office had found nearly a week before. Back then, Rex had had time to view the rigid bodies in Ætheria's morgue. At first, he had been horrified by what he thought to be monstrous deformations, but now he began to wonder. If the Cthonians had been living down here—in this dense air—for the same amount of time the

Ætherians had been living in the thin stratosphere, this might explain their difference in height. In just the few minutes Rex had breathed without his mask, he felt strong enough to run dozens of miles without stopping—and with each breath, he felt stronger. If that were so, then generations of humans spending hundreds of years in this life-giving environment would surely produce much larger and stronger creatures. If not for the acid rain from the Welcans cloud, Rex imagined this world could be the lushest imaginable—far more so than anything the Ætherians could cultivate under the protective biodomes of the gardening islands above the clouds. And the presence of the cloud explained why the Cthonians were so pale and the Ætherians so dark. Even though the sun was now up, it remained hidden behind the cloud, filling the world with nothing but a dull yellowish glow. For the Ætherians, however, they had been exposed nonstop to intense ultraviolet rays from the sun for hundreds of years, whereas the Cthonians had probably not seen direct sunlight in nearly a millennium.

"Rex, does she look like the others? The ones you saw? In the morgue?" Yoné asked without looking at him. "I never saw them, but I was told you did. By . . . someone." She looked away, as if feeling she'd said too much.

At Yoné's words, Aral gave a start. Rex also felt a spark of alarm to think Yoné knew much more about him than she let on. But before he could process what it all meant, Aral turned her attention to Rex. Her eyes widened and scanned every detail of his face, lingering on his drooping left eye and the paralyzed left corner of his mouth. At the sight of this strange Cthonian staring at him, Rex squirmed uncomfortably and looked around.

"Rex . . . " Aral muttered. "Your name is Rex," she said more as a statement than a question. She spoke with a thick, strange accent that was guttural and resonant.

Rex took a step back. The Cthonian's fixation

on him was unnerving, even though she seemed to be about his age. Still, his thoughts froze under her gaze, and he forgot what Yoné had just asked. Seeing his confusion, Yoné moved forward and spoke more insistently.

"You, Cthonian, why are you here? Your name is Aral, you said?"

"You," Aral said, ignoring Yoné. Her eyes remained riveted on Rex's. "Your eye. Your face. Rex . . . ?" Aral squinted and seemed to be recalling some memory. Her expression was one of wonder mixed with shock.

"What?" Yoné said. She looked back and forth between Rex and Aral.

"You," Aral repeated, inching toward Rex. "Who *are* you? They called you . . . Rex?"

Rex furrowed his brow, his sense of unease growing. He felt his heart beat faster, and a cold sweat cover his face and neck.

"*We're* going to ask the questions here!" Yoné snapped, anger growing in her voice. "Did you know about this attack? Were you part of it? What happened here?! Tell us!"

Aral ignored Yoné's questions.

"What is your mother's name?" Aral asked. "Where does she live?"

A visible wave of astonishment rippled through the scouts. Some gasped. Some faltered in holding their Stær guns. Some turned and looked back and forth between Aral, Yoné, and Rex. Yoné gaped. Rex stepped back, his mind swirling as if in a dream. Forgotten dreams and imagined memories of his mother flashed through his imagination. As if instinctively, he reached his hand down to his AeroGel suit, where he'd tucked his mother's photograph six days before. Though his suit was thin, he couldn't make out the photo's shape through the super-insulated material. He inched his hand into his pocket, his fingers probing for the small square piece of photographic paper. Its corners met his searching fingertips, and he grasped her image and pinched, afraid to let it go.

"Why are you asking about him?" Yoné said, gripping her Stær gun tighter. "What do you care about his mother?"

"She's gone," Rex said in a flat tone. He too was now oblivious to Yoné and the others. He felt something strange when speaking to Aral—as if he suspected she might hold some clue to understanding his own life.

"What?" Aral asked.

"She left when I was born." There was something about Aral's insistent stare and seeming recognition of who he was that made Rex trust her . . . or at least *want* to trust her.

"How long ago?"

"Sixteen years."

"What's her name?" Aral asked. "Because . . . I mean, well, I should tell you—and all of you, really—that there is an Ætherian here . . . living with us. And she's been down here for fifteen or sixteen years. She got here just before I was born. She fled from Ætheria. Her name is Máire Himmel."

"Mom!?" Rex let out a cry of alarm and disbelief at hearing his mother's name. His tone betrayed his thoughts: *What are you talking about?* His eye stung, and his stomach cramped. He pulled his hands over his chest, at the same time yanking the photo from his pocket. Realizing what he held, he turned the photographic paper around to show Máire's grainy face to Aral. He stepped forward, his arm extended, bringing the photo to within a foot of Aral's eyes.

"Is this who you mean?" he said, his voice wavering. "Is this her? The . . . Ætherian?"

Aral reached forward and gingerly slid the photo from his fingers. She brought it closer and squinted, her nose scrunching up in concentration. No sooner had her vision focused on the image than her eyes widened and her eyebrows raised in astonishment. She lowered the photo and looked at Rex.

"This *is* her. She came down for asylum before I can remember. She was my teacher two or three years ago. She teaches all kids at our complex about Ætherian history and civilization. But she would never talk about Ætheria without talking about her son. She said your name many times: 'Rex—Rex, the baby I had to leave behind. And who had had an accident at birth that paralyzed half of his face.' It's *you*."

Rex moved before he could process his actions. He lunged forward and grabbed Aral by the shoulders. A shocked expression crossed her face, but it was an expression mixed with heartfelt satisfaction—relief, even, at some mystery that had just been solved.

"What?!" Rex shouted. "What are you talking about? Do you know my mom?! Is she here? Don't mess with me! Tell me the truth!" The many stories his foster dad had told him over the years of his mom's leaving flashed through his mind. His dad had never given details. He had never explained why. Maybe he hadn't known? That was unlikely. He was, after all, one of the most powerful people in Ætheria as head of Energy and Survival. But then the thought occurred: the Ætherian High

Command had always hoarded oxygen; his dad had always talked about there being "no missteps in Ætheria;" he'd heard about the Tossings; he'd been arrested and forced to join the Ætherian Cover Force with no other explanation than he "was special." Could his mother have been persecuted and forced to flee? And could Aral bring him closer to her?

Yoné stepped forward and grabbed Rex's arms. She pulled him away from the Cthonian and turned him to face her.

"Your mom?" Yoné stammered to Rex. And then to Aral, "What else do you know?"

"Yes, where is she?!" Rex blurted out, turning back to Aral and ignoring Yoné. The Cthonian stepped back and glanced at the scouts, who surrounded her but seemed unsure of what to do or think. Aral's eyes rested on Yoné. Aral's expression seemed to be asking permission to speak. She shifted her regard to Rex.

"It *must* be your mother." Aral narrowed her eyes

and examined Rex's features, as if trying to convince herself of who she was looking at—even though everything fit: his eye, his mouth, the picture, the dates, the name . . . "She even looks like you as well. Or rather, you look like her. She is with my people," Aral finally said.

Rex wiped his eye.

"Where?"

"That way," Aral said, pointing toward the west. "She's been working in water rationing and teaching. She's been doing that since she came, I think."

As Aral spoke, Rex's mind quickly forgot about his mission—about his orders. With what was coming to light, he now could care less about searching the wreckage of Tátea's Power Works. He could care less about repairing the Proboscis. All he wanted now was to know—for certain—if the person Aral was referring to was really his mom. And if it was, how could he get to her? A surge of tingling, long-lost emotion filled him. It was a mix of excitement, sadness, and the hope that he might be able to have a family—a real family.

"But why are you out here?" Yoné interrupted. "You say 'that way,' but how far is that? Where is that?"

Aral took a deep breath.

"We live two days out. I was part of a team sent to get water. Our aquifer's all run out, and our reserves are drying up. We always knew you were here. And Máire told us you had water. So we came, really, to find you. The Ætherians. To see if you could help us. Here," Aral pointed to the still smoldering remains of Tátea's Power Works.

Yoné blinked. She looked at the other scouts.

"We are from up there," Yoné said and pointed to the Welcans cloud. "What happened here? Why did you attack us?" Anger bubbled up in her words.

Aral shook her head.

"I didn't. I didn't want this. I wanted to stop it. I was with a team who came to try to contact you. But our general . . . his son was killed—fell from

above. And then Brondl—that's our general—
starting saying that *you* were stealing our water.
He thought you were trying to kill *us*. But he was
wrong. Can I show you something?" Aral said
before Yoné could answer. "It will explain better
than me," Aral said, nodding in the direction of the
transport vehicle.

"Can you take me to her?" Rex asked.

At Rex's words, Aral swung her head toward him
and narrowed her eyes. But before she could answer,
Yoné interrupted.

"Rex! Hold on . . . you've got . . . we've got
something to do, here, and you know it. First things
first. Let's see what's going on here. We'll deal with
what she's saying about the Ætherian in a minute.
But first," she turned to Aral, "why did your people
attack us?"

"You don't understand," Aral said. "Follow me,
and I'll show you. Over there. In the airship."

"You just wait," Yoné said. "Why were you here?

In this mess? We saw you snooping around. What were you doing here . . . by yourself?"

Aral looked around again, her eyes focused as if she were looking for something.

"Before we—they, I mean—cut that pipe, we had a command post here with forty of us. My general is the one who attacked. But I thought . . . I mean . . . anyway, when they blew it, something exploded—something much bigger than what was supposed to happen, I think. Something in the ground—gas or something. All our general wanted to do was cut your pipe, but the explosion ignited a gas in the pipe that shot all the way up. When that happened, I ran to the airship to hide. And when I came out, everything was destroyed. There must've been some gas underground that blew everything up. When you came, I was looking for survivors— survivors, and water. Really, I was looking for anything I could use to try to get back. I found some food and water in one of our locker tanks over there, but I couldn't breathe because of all the dust. That's why you saw me with the mask . . . "

"A mask? Just for the dust?" Rex piped in. "So you don't need masks down here to breathe?"

Aral looked puzzled.

"No. Why would we? Of course we can breathe. Why wouldn't we be able to? We all can. We've always been able to . . . at least as far as I can remember."

The team of scouts exchanged glances. Their strained faces betrayed the whirlwind of their conflicting thoughts. All their lives they'd been told by the Ætherian Council that the air on Cthonia was unbreathable, yet here was a Cthonian telling them that all of her people could breathe just fine.

"Wait, wait, wait," Yoné said. "You said you wanted to get back. Back where?"

"Back home. I'll tell you more. But right now let me show you something that will explain. Please."

"Okay, but wait," Yoné said, walking around to Aral's back. Once there, Yoné reached forward and grabbed the back of Aral's black shirt in her left fist, while she lifted her Stær gun with her right. She pointed the weapon directly at Aral's gangly legs.

"I've got a Stær gun pointed at you. If you make one quick movement—anything faster than a slow walk—I'll shoot. You'll be hit with enough electricity to knock you out. So no tricks."

While Yoné was speaking, Aral kept her head tilted to the side so that she could keep her eye on her smaller captor. She nodded.

"You can trust me," Aral said. "I promise. Let me help."

Aral moved forward. Rex stepped to Yoné's right and kept an eye on the Cthonian.

As they moved, Rex was transfixed by Aral's taller body and pale skin. He thought he could make out light blue veins under her pallor. *If someone looked like that back in Ætheria,* he thought, *they would be thought sick and sent for care.* As the Cthonian moved, he realized she was taking steps that were—for her—unnaturally small. Her demeanor seemed relaxed, and Rex had a calm feeling of reassurance. He felt he could trust her. She hadn't resisted. She hadn't played any tricks . . . yet. And his mother?

The other Ætherians inched along to either side of Yoné and Aral, keeping their Stær guns trained on their prisoner. They too seemed both relaxed and tense at the same time—relaxed because of the energizing air that they were breathing and the relief of knowing there to be no danger from the atmosphere, and tense for fear that this Cthonian might trick them into an ambush.

The closer the team drew to the airship, the more Rex's attention shifted from Aral to the bizarre contraption. Back on Ætheria, many of the domes and houses had ceilings and walls that were translucent. This allowed electricity demands to drop because the buildings would absorb the light and heat from the sun's uninterrupted daylight rays. This machine, however, was of solid metal, not unlike that used in the Proboscis or the stratoneum struts that held

Ætheria aloft. The entire airship shone silver in the morning light. As they approached, Rex noticed the machine's surface was riddled with what appeared to be small rivets or bolts holding sheets of metal together. But what had been a smooth surface was now dented by the debris that had tumbled down from the stratosphere and crashed into Cthonia, ricocheting up and onto the machine. The airship was still intact, but damaged. *Still*, Rex wondered. *How could this be? How could this thing possibly fly? How could this contraption get over its enormous weight to get up into the sky?* He eyed the motors with curiosity mixed with suspicion. Back in Ætheria, he had never seen any machines that compact. Even though each motor was large enough for a person to fit inside, they were much smaller than the turbines and water filtration systems he'd seen back on Tátea.

As they approached, the dozen or so animals Rex had seen earlier vanished behind the airship. Just as he'd stared at Aral in wonder, his curiosity flared at the sight of these otherworldly, hooved creatures that towered over all of them.

"There," Aral said, pointing. Rex followed her outstretched hand, which indicated a smooth-cornered, rectangular oval hatch on the side, just down from and behind the glass housing that must've held the machine's operators. "In here."

"Okay," Yoné said to Aral. "Let's go in, but remember what I said." As they followed the Cthonian in, Rex noticed that Yoné's hand was shaking.

Aral paused at the edge of the airship's door. Rex couldn't tell if she was hesitating or if she was trying to give Yoné a chance to peek in. Aral placed her hands on either side of the frame and leaned forward, pausing once more. Yoné stood on her toes and glanced in. The other scouts huddled close behind her, but not so close that they wouldn't be able to use their Stær guns in case Aral tried something.

"Ready?" Aral said.

"Yes. Go ahead."

Moving so that Yoné wouldn't lose her grip on her prisoner, Aral pulled herself up and into the airship's body. Rex noticed she had to duck to go through. The door was too short. For Yoné, however, the size was just right. The top edge left a margin of more than six inches. Rex and the others followed.

Though the airship had appeared huge from the outside, Rex didn't get a sense of the size until he had stepped through the hatch.

From the inside, the vehicle reminded him a little of the transport tubes that connected Ætheria's buildings. Ribs of metal stretched up both sides, giving him the impression of being in some giant animal. Unlike the transport tubes, however, the airship's interior was metallic and opaque, and much, much larger. There were no seats, only a crisscross of mesh that ran up and down both sides. What looked like thick cargo straps dangled from the ceiling and the walls, their ends metallic buckles.

To the left, the airship's body stretched backwards, narrowing as it neared the tail. To the right, another open hatch led to a small room filled with hundreds of controls, buttons, and small screens. Two cushy seats were mounted facing forward and toward the airship's windows. Whoever sat there would have direct access to the controls. Rex wondered if that was where you piloted the machine.

"Here," Aral scooted over to the far side of the machine. Yoné followed close behind. When she'd reached the mesh, Aral kneeled and scooped some papers from the floor. She stood and handed them to Yoné.

"I had these in my hand when I ran away." She glanced at the papers. "There are two things here," Aral said. "Our command's orders and a transcript. We sent six people up that tube. When they spoke, it was recorded here. We thought they were dead, because these fell down in ComPods. Here. Read for yourself. This tells us exactly what they were saying right before . . . right before we lost contact for good."

Yoné took the papers and glanced at the others before lowering eyes to the text. She read quickly, her lips mouthing the words. She skimmed through the pages, snapping each out of the way when she'd reached the bottom of the page.

When she was done she looked up.

"So what?" Yoné asked.

"When he read those, and when his son's body fell down, our general planted the explosives. But then this came to us." Aral pointed at the second sheet. Yoné read.

```
Command has received your request to
sever the tube. We cannot support this
action. You will desist immediately.
Explosives are dated and Ætherian infor-
mant reports that one of the pipes is
filled with explosive cthoneum gas that
is being piped upward. The slight-
est spark could trigger a devastating
```

explosion, potentially igniting massive underground detonation. **DO NOT PROCEED.**

"Wait, so *he* was trying to declare war on us," Yoné hissed.

Aral said nothing. She kept her eyes fixed on Yoné's.

"All your people wanted was help . . . " Yoné continued. "But us, we, we thought you were attacking us, the Cthonians, I mean, and so . . . " her voice trailed off. "We've both got it wrong. Both the Ætherians *and* the Cthonians." Yoné let the papers fall to the floor. Rex watched them flutter down, their movement reminding him of Tátea's destroyed Power Works as the building plummeted through the Welcans cloud to its destruction on Cthonia.

"We've got to set this right. And quick, before any other mistakes are made."

EIGHT

YONÉ TURNED HER BACK ON ARAL AND THE other scouts. She stepped through the airship's hatch and outside. The others followed without a word.

Even though the rain had stopped, the ground was a muddy, glistening mess. Acidic water pooled up in the cluster of iridescent footprints the scouts had made in their pursuit of Aral, who now stood with them. Off to the right of the rubble from the explosion, four or five of those massive animals moseyed together. They stood close to each other as if keeping each other warm, but they ignored the people emerging from the damaged airship.

Yoné stopped before the rubble and contemplated the scene of destruction. She put her hands on her hips and said nothing for several minutes. The others stopped behind her, holding their eyes on her with bated breath. She suddenly turned and faced Aral.

"I wonder . . . " Yoné said, turning back to the animals.

"Yes?"

Yoné turned around and looked at the guy wires and stratoneum struts reaching up from the ground. The Welcans cloud churned and boiled above them. It seemed ready to release another torrent of acidic rain on the barren landscape.

"Look," Yoné said, turning back to the group. "There are twelve of us—thirteen, I mean, with you," she nodded toward Aral. "What we should do is split into two groups. Five of us go back up to Ætheria and inform the Council of what we've found, while the others head to your people on those animals. That seems the best way, because we've got to hurry. Those who'd go back up would inform the ACF of what we've found: first, that we can breathe down here; and second, about you. Only thing is," she looked around as if taking inventory of the gear the scouts carried on their backs. "There's no way we'd make it. How far did you say it was? Two days?"

"Yes."

"Hmm." Yoné looked down and rubbed her chin, lost in thought.

"As far as water and food goes," Aral said, "there are some reserve cans here—maybe one hundred liters each. And we have food in some containers that weren't completely destroyed. We could load up the extra eqūs and bring them with us." She looked around. Several of the animals lingered a dozen yards to the front of the airship. Their noses were to the ground, sniffing for food. "If we *can* make it back to the CCC, there's food and water there. Though our water is running short."

"CCC?" Yoné asked.

"Cthonian Cave Complex. That's where we live. It's a colony buried in a cave." Aral thought. "What choice do we have?" the Cthonian said. "If we go up there, we're in the same boat, right? Didn't you say your people thought we were spies? You're here, aren't you? So why not do what you say? You send some people back up, and the others come with me. When we get to the CCC, I go in first and explain. That you're peacemakers . . . If I'm with you, you should be fine. I am one of them, remember."

A silence fell over the group.

"Right now, I don't see any other choice," Yoné finally said. "Let's do it."

"Okay," the Cthonian said. "Have you ever ridden an equūs before?" Seeing the Ætherians' confused looks, she added, "These animals are called equūs—they're how we get around down here."

Rex's hips screamed. His ribs ached. His rear end throbbed as the massive, muscular creature moved up and down in a steady rhythm, its shoulder and back muscles flexing with unbelievable power under its sweaty, glistening hide. He'd been on the eqūs for several hours now, and despite the pain and strangeness of the feel of riding an actual, live animal, he felt he was getting used to its movements. What he wasn't getting used to was the nonstop itching and watering that attacked his eyes, and the irresistible, nonstop urge to sneeze. Growing up in the stratospheric Ætheria, he'd never felt this much pain in his lungs, his throat, and his mouth and nose before. At first he wondered if Yoné had been right about the Cthonian air—if it was finally getting to him and causing him to suffocate. But his reaction had only begun once he'd gotten on the eqūs, and he'd had his mask off long before that.

The group had been riding at a steady pace for several hours. Shortly after Aral and Yoné had discussed riding back to the CCC, five of the scouts headed back to the descent pods while the team mounted and spurred their steeds. As they did, Aral could not help laughing as the Ætherians struggled with the animals, which seemed massive compared to their smaller figures. She had to walk to each of the scouts and push them up, work their feet into the stirrups, and show them how to hold the reins. And then they were off.

For the first time since he'd landed on the Cthonian surface, Rex noticed he was thirsty. Throat-achingly thirsty. He reached down and pulled his water tube from his shoulder strap, where it remained hooked into his gear apparatus. The tube then disappeared into his backpack, where a four-liter bladder of water stayed cool from the heat. Four liters. Enough for two days. Perhaps. Maybe three, if they avoided walking themselves by staying perched on the animals. As he sipped through the tube's mouthpiece, he turned and looked at the eqūs Aral had loaded with the vats of water. It was three eqūs back.

He turned back around and let his eyes settle on Yoné's shoulders. Ahead of her, Aral's tall, lanky form led the group. For the first time, Rex noticed her hair floated at least a full yard down between her shoulder blades and toward her waist. But as the desert wind leaned into them from the left side, her hair blew up in the wind. Rex marveled at how clean—how well cared for—it looked. He also wondered at her age. She looked sixteen, just like him.

And then the thought struck him: *What are we doing?* Within just a few hours of landing in a foreign world, he'd discovered that everything he'd ever learned about the Cthonian atmosphere was wrong. At least one Cthonian was not hostile. And rather than just make some observations and head back up like the other three scouts, here he was, heading into the lion's den. His head spun.

The next few hours were uneventful. Rolling

dunes, drab salt flats, and the occasional hill jutting out from the plain countryside offered little to look at. Soon everything seemed to blend into one bland mass of grayish-beige, interrupted only by the lumbering dark forms of the equs.

Rex blinked and rubbed his eyes. He looked up at the rumbling Welcans cloud. No, he hadn't been mistaken. Night was falling.

"We should stop," Aral said, her voice cutting crisp and clear across the flat expanse. "For the equs. And we should sleep, too." As her words trailed off, she turned and stopped her equs, its body perpendicular to the others'. He gaped at the animal's bulging brown eye, the circular white indicating that the equs was staring in wonder—or terror—at the Ætherians.

"Where?" Rex found himself asking before deferring to Yoné. "Here? In the open?"

Yoné just looked at him over her left shoulder.

"No other choice," Aral said, spurring her equs ahead a few paces. "We tie the equs together. As long as we stay with them, they won't wander off. Looks like the ground here is drier."

She led her animal in a wide circle, as if marking off the area where they would sleep.

As for the scouts, they held their eqūs steady. Everyone but Yoné drank from their water tubes. Some of the scouts exchanged apprehensive words.

"Shhh!" Aral snapped, cutting them off. Rex turned. The Cthonian suddenly seemed anxious— all of her muscles ready to fight or flee. She darted her eyes around the horizon. She seemed to be looking for something—but something that was invisible to the naked eye.

"Do you hear that?"

NINE

REX'S BODY WENT TENSE. HE JERKED HIS head around, trying to make out what Aral had heard. But apart from his own breathing and the desert wind cutting across the sand, he heard nothing. He glanced at Yoné and the others. All of the scouts were hunched over and nervous, but they scanned the darkening landscape with jerky rabbit eyes looking for danger. Only Aral seemed to know what was happening. Her eyes settled on the western horizon. Her hand worked its way up to the pommel of her eqūs's saddle. She fingered it as if trying to decide whether to mount again or to stay with her feet planted. Rex slid back up to his eqūs and tightened his fingers around the reins.

And then he heard it. It was a sound unlike any he'd ever heard before. A buzz—no, a low rumble—something mechanical, something big, something powerful, and something that wasn't yet visible. It was coming from the west. He turned his head to the source of the hidden noise. The other scouts did the same. They'd all heard it.

As the sound grew in volume, Aral became agitated. Rex saw that her shoulders were heaving up and down as her breathing quickened.

The sound now had a high-pitched quality—almost like a scream or whistle on top of the rumble, which was quickly growing to a roar. It sounded like some sort of machine—an engine, maybe—but what did Rex know? The only engine he'd ever heard was that of the Power Works facility on Tátea; and then, he'd only heard that when he'd been about twelve, when his foster dad had taken him to visit the complex with his school group.

"It's them," Aral said, mounting. "They're coming."

"Who?" Yoné snapped. Rex's blood went cold and his heartbeat accelerated.

"Listen," Aral continued, holding up her hand to point to the west. "They must be sending support. From the CCC. That's another airship, coming this way."

"An airship? Like the thing we saw back there?" Rex said.

"Yes." Aral cocked her head and listened. "There's only one. That's all we've got, anyway: two planes. But they're flying low."

Yoné got back on her eqūs. Rex and the other scouts did likewise. Yoné's head snapped around. She scanned the Welcans cloud and the landscape.

"Do you think they'll see us?"

"I don't know. It's getting dark, but they probably have infrared. Still, I don't even know if they'll be using it . . . or if they'll even think to be looking for anything on the ground before they get to the outpost site."

"What's infrared?" Rex asked.

Aral turned and faced him.

"It's a type of camera that lets them see body heat, even in the dark. So even at night, they'd be able to see us, unless we were hidden in a cave or something."

Yoné stood tall and scanned the desert. All around, only flat, featureless terrain was to be seen.

"There's nowhere to hide," she said.

"But we don't want to hide; we want to talk to them . . . " Aral's voice trailed off. "Let's stay closer. Maybe then our heat will be enough for them to see us. But I don't know how fast they're going . . . "

"Okay, let's do it! Scouts!" Yoné snapped. The Ætherians edged in closer, but not so close that they were touching.

Off toward the west, about two or three miles away, two white lights were visible. The airship. The lights were low, perhaps halfway between the ground and the Welcans cloud, and the machine was hurtling towards them. As it approached, Rex could make out a red and a green light—the green on the right, the red on the left. It was heading toward the destroyed Cthonian encampment and the Tátea Power Works remains. What would they think when they discovered the desolation? What would they do? Would they find the pods and try an ascent up to Ætheria? After all, with the Proboscis destroyed, they wouldn't be able to come up the same way they did before . . .

Rex held his breath. His hands trembled. There, on the eqūs, with his head nearly ten feet off the ground, he felt exposed to this mechanical behemoth that was unlike anything he'd ever seen in Ætheria. His emotions swirled between wonder at the technological marvel and sheer terror. How did it stay aloft? How was it powered? Would the airship attack them? Why? Or would it try to make peaceful contact? How fast was it going? Why didn't they have these on Ætheria? Would the people in the airship see them on the ground? Were they even looking?

The airship's roar grew and grew. It was fewer than a hundred yards away horizontally, though it was at least a thousand feet up. Instinctively, Rex raised his hands to his ears. He'd never heard anything this loud. Even the whipping stratospheric winds in Ætheria paled in comparison to the screaming released by this monster.

Rex looked down, trying to spot the others. In the dark, all he could make out was a few hazy forms. From his position, he couldn't tell where they were looking—up, or at the others, or down . . .

The airship approached and was soon directly overhead. A numbing sense of awe filled Rex, as it became clear the pilots hadn't seen them. The machine was going to fly over and disappear in the east. Relief filling his body, Rex was now transfixed. Though he could only make out its vague silhouette in the dark, he could see that it appeared identical to the one back at the Cthonian camp: two large wings with hulking engines clinging onto the sides. Rex plunged his fingers into his ears as the airship passed by, because the screaming roar increased to a painful level once the engines' exhaust faced them.

The airship snarled past, sending Rex's eqūs into a panic. Rex jerked his hands from his ears and pulled back on the lurching animal. The roar racked his body. The eqūs reared up on its hind legs, threatening to throw Rex to the ground. He lurched forward and threw his arms around the animal's thick, muscular neck. The eqūs came down with a jolt onto all four legs. It didn't rear up again, but it danced with its front legs as if warning Rex that it was preparing to buck him off. Rex worked his way back to a sitting position and once again pulled hard against the reins.

"Shhhhhhh," he hissed in as comforting a tone as he could muster, despite his new fear of being tossed from the animal and injured in the fall. "Shhhhh . . ."

Amid angry snorts, the eqūs relaxed. Rex let go of the reins with his left hand and stroked the animal's neck, trying to soothe it.

"Shhhhhh . . . "

And then something happened. Something caught Rex's eye off to the right. The airship . . . its lights . . . Rex sat up and turned to face the Cthonian aircraft, whose lights had been fading into the distance.

It was turning around.

It was coming back.

TEN

AS THE AIRSHIP TURNED, REX WAS STUNNED to notice it came to almost a complete standstill midair, hovered, and then rotated its nose in their direction. From this distance, he couldn't tell what about the machine's engines was allowing it this feat. Not only was it dark and the airship far away, but the moment it faced them, powerful spotlights snapped on and pointed to the ground and at an angle. The machine lumbered forward with a renewed roar and plunged to about three hundred feet. Two round swaths of ground one hundred feet in diameter now glowed a quarter mile in front of the beast as its spotlights combed the ground.

Looking for us, Rex thought.

With the airship approaching, Rex's panic stirred once more. Without thinking, he spurred his equs ahead and led it the sixty or so yards to where Yoné stood stock-still, eyeing the screaming metal behemoth with a mixture of wonder and terror. In the same movement, he withdrew his Stær gun from his holster, though he pulled the weapon instinctively. Not only had he damaged it by dropping it into the mud earlier, but what could a jolt of one hundred thousand volts realistically do to a flying machine of this size?

"Yoné!" Rex screamed as his equs reached within twenty feet. As if hypnotized by the spectacle of the massive airship approaching amid a howl of engines and what was quickly becoming a sandstorm of wash thrown up by the now upward-facing engine, she didn't react at first. Rex pulled his equs close enough to be able to grab her arm.

"Yoné!" he shouted again. She turned and stared at him with wide, terrified eyes. In her surprise, she also withdrew her Stær gun and held it ready. Seeing the weapon sent a wave of nervous energy through Rex. Seeing this, the other scouts also drew their weapons.

"Look at those engines," she said, her voice inaudible under the din. Rex was only able to make out her words between reading her lips and thinking the same thing. The machine was able to hover and fly in most directions because the jet engines on either side rotated, sending the propulsion backwards, down, and any direction in between.

"What are we going to do?!" Rex screamed again.

"Wait!" A massive hand clamped down on his right shoulder, causing him to jump. He didn't have to turn to know that it was Aral. Still, he wheeled around to see that she and the remaining scouts had ridden back close together. Their gaping eyes jerked back and forth between Yoné, Aral, and the airship, which was now hovering less than a quarter mile above and in front of them. Like some night-marish photograph, it hovered, its blinding white headlights trained on the assembled group of scouts. Rex's body tingled from fear, but the roar of the two jet engines overpowered his own thoughts.

Without talking to any of the scouts, Aral eased her eqūs forward and away from the group. She kept her head craned upwards. She stared at the air-ship and lifted her hands. At first, she shielded her eyes from the blinding light. Then she moved both of them about, apparently trying to make some sort of hand signals to whoever was piloting the craft.

Rex wondered what the pilots could see from up there. Clearly they could see the entire group, but would they be able to make out that one of them was a Cthonian, while the others were Ætherians? From that distance, would the pilots be able to see that Aral was much paler and taller than they? Would they even recognize her personally? What did they know about what had happened at the command post? Was she using some sort of sign language that they recognized?

For what seemed like minutes, the airship hovered, its massive glowing eyes sizing them up. It seemed to be thinking, mulling over what to do.

Aral finished signaling and lowered her hands, resting them on her thighs. Rex could see her shoulders heaving from her breathing. She too must've been frightened . . . by her own people.

After a few more moments passed, Aral grabbed her eqūs's reins and coaxed the animal backwards. When she was within earshot of the scouts, she turned and cupped her free hand over her mouth.

"It's okay, I think! They should know who I am! I tried to tell them that you . . . "

She never finished her sentence. With no warning, Rex's eqūs whinnied and bolted, causing him to thrash about wildly as he tried to maintain his balance. In his agitation, Rex's malfunctioning Stær gun popped with a flash, sending a net of electrified barbs flying upward in the direction of the airship.

At the sound of his gun, he dropped the weapon and latched onto the saddle's pommel with both hands. In the glaring white of the airship's spotlights, Rex shouted something at the animal, but he didn't know exactly how to calm the creature.

Within seconds of Rex's Stær gun's misfiring, bright red blasts erupted from the sides of the airship, from somewhere under the wings.

The pilots must've thought that Rex was shooting at them. Without hesitation, they began shooting back. A hailstorm of bullets rained down upon the group, sending volleys of sand twenty feet high and covering them with dirt and gritty debris. If the sound of the machine's engines was deafening, the popping of the explosions was skull-shattering.

"It's a mistake! They think you shot at them!" Aral shouted over the motors. But before she was midway through her sentence, Yoné's screeching voice interrupted the Cthonian.

"Aaaaahhhhhh!" From Rex's left, Yoné screamed

in pain, and her body flew over the back of the eqūs. Rex looked over and saw her lying facedown in the grayish sand, a pool of dark red swelling from underneath her. Within seconds of her falling, the pack on her back began blinking and beeping wildly. Red and green lights flickered on its left side. At first pulsing chaotically, they soon flashed at an ever-slowing pace until they settled on a dim red glow. When they stopped flickering, the pod emitted a high-pitched alarm.

Yoné was dead.

Rex stared at his former Point's body, his eyes resting on the beeping pod.

Oh, my God, he thought. *They're going to know up top. This will send back one of the pods!*

More explosions. More sand. More panic. More screaming.

"My God!"

"They're killing us!"

"Run!"

The remaining scouts screamed as one. The eqūs

reared back and whinnied in terror. To keep from falling over, Rex leaned forward and clutched his eqūs's reins. Everything around him was a blur of light, sand puffs, explosions, and spurts of red as the airborne Cthonians' bullets tore into his team members' bodies. As they fell, their blinking and flashing pods cast eerie, almost sparkling stars across the gray, lifeless sand. The message was being sent to the descent pods, which were no doubt carrying the warning back up to Ætheria—the message that the first skirmishes of a war were under way.

Rex looked around and saw that Aral was unhurt. She seemed just as panicked as the others, and in that moment any suspicion that Rex may have had about Aral's trustworthiness vanished. She was clearly a pariah in her own land—an outcast slated for destruction. Just like the invading Ætherians.

"Get back to the wires!" Rex screamed over to Aral. Her eyes locked on his and she furrowed her brow in confusion. "The pod just sent a signal up to

Ætheria. They're gonna know something's wrong! Back there!" he pointed to the direction they came. "We have to get back to our pods and get up, now!" A thought suddenly flashed through his mind— something that Aral had said earlier when they'd first gone into the wrecked airship. *The airship won't be able to follow us into the wires!* "We have to go!" As he turned, he wondered if the five scouts had made it up yet and if so, what message they'd delivered. Would the Ætherians be sending others down? *No*, Rex thought, *we've used all the descent pods! And the Welcans cloud is probably still too violent to send anyone down in the harnesses . . .*

"Weave as you run!" Aral screamed, pulling her equs near Rex's. "Don't run in a straight line! And not together!" She screamed so loud, the veins in her neck bulged. She glared at the others to make sure they heard her. "They can't aim for you that way! You're smaller and more agile, so don't let them get you! Now *go*!"

With that, she too spurred her equs into a run.

Rex followed, pulling his animal's reins off to the right for a while, and then to the left for a while, and then back to the right.

As the animals gained speed, the remaining scouts and Aral soon passed under the hovering aircraft, which rotated dumbly as they passed. With the engines' roar now behind him, Rex stood in his stirrups and kept his body low to the animal's back. His thighs burned with the effort, and every nerve in his body awaited the searing hot pain of the bullet that would rocket down from the Cthonian aircraft and kill him as an enemy.

ELEVEN

THE BULLETS CAME, BUT NOT ONE THAT would kill Rex.

The group fled and swerved through the night, which had completely fallen. The only light came from the two spotlights on the lumbering aircraft behind them, and the lightning-like blasts of its wing cannons. In the terror of hurtling through the dark, dodging left then right at the mercy of the eqūs's senses, Rex didn't have time to process Yoné's death, nor anything else that was happening. All that mattered now was not getting shot.

As the eqūs's hooves pounded over the Cthonian

desert sands, bullets whizzed by like invisible missiles, and bursts of sand erupted all around, frightening the eqūs, who neighed and whinnied in protest, but Rex's heels were unrelenting. He kicked the eqūs's sides violently, urging it to go faster, faster, faster . . . The faster the eqūs ran, the slower the aircraft seemed to hover behind them, its massive engines throwing up blinding clouds of sand and searing exhaust. Viewed from a distance, the scene must've appeared comical: a warplane that could cover miles in mere seconds creeping along at a snail's pace, its cannons targeting a ragtag group of scouts and eqūs, hurtling across the dark sands below.

"Ahhhh!" some scouts screamed off to Rex's right. He turned his head but couldn't tell who'd been hit. Their pods' high-pitched alarms squealed through the night. If the ACF back home didn't know the scouts were under attack, they would know soon enough. And then what?

Only three scouts remained—three scouts, and Aral.

Rex couldn't tell how long he and the others had been riding—ten minutes? Thirty? But two things happened that forced his panicked thoughts into a new idea: *How much longer can this last?*

First, the gunfire ceased. The aircraft still followed them at its low altitude, its white spotlights lighting the way forward like two massive headlights. Was it out of ammunition? Had the pilots changed their strategy? Or was there some other trap in store for them?

Second, Rex's eqūs began to falter. For a lengthy stretch of land, the animal had kept a powerful and unwavering pace, its honed muscles propelling the two forward faster than Rex had ever moved. But now it slowed, it snorted, it stumbled but regained its footing, it whinnied in irritation and exhaustion. Rex had never ridden an eqūs before today, but he could now sense that he was, in fact, dealing with a sentient creature and not a machine.

"Come on, boy, come on," he whispered, as if expecting the equs to hear and understand him . . . as if his words of encouragement would be enough to rouse the animal out of its rut. Rex leaned forward and placed his palm on the equs's shoulder. He jerked it back, surprised at the thick rivulets of sweat that coursed down the steed's back.

Feeling his hand, the equs let out another snort and slowed to a trot. It was failing him.

From behind, Rex heard a shift in the airship's roar—the engines' scream switched from a low-pitched rumble to a high-pitched howl. Was something wrong? He turned over his shoulder and saw the aircraft no longer moved forward. It had paused and now hovered midair, about two hundred feet from the ground. It was lowering itself to land. *What's going on?* Huge swirls of sand blew out underneath the airship's exhaust wash. Rex covered his eyes to protect them from the stinging sand. He turned back towards the front of the equs.

Then he understood.

His silhouette now growing in length because of the airship's descending lights, Rex made out the vertical network of guy wires announcing their approach to the original Cthonian command post site and the Power Works' remains. The airship had landed to avoid flying into the wires, which would have downed the craft. But where was the damaged airship? Had it been removed? Stunned, Rex scanned the horizon for the wreckage, but all he saw was hundreds of wires stretching up from the ground and at a slight angle as they climbed up to the Ætherian islands far above.

He looked off to the left and realized his mistake. Off in the distance, at ten o'clock and about three hundred yards away, trickles of flickering orange seeped their way through the dark. The remains of Tátea's Power Works. The remaining scouts and Aral had returned south of the wreckage site. He squinted and looked farther to the left, where the other airship had landed; only darkness greeted him. But he knew it was there, slumbering.

"Over there!" he shouted to Aral and the two other scouts. "We're off place! The pods are over there!"

Allowing his equs to move more deliberately to avoid the guy wires, Rex pulled the left rein to direct the animal closer to the wreckage. He knew the pods were due east of the rubble, and he didn't want to risk getting lost in the obscure jungle of wires and stratoneum struts, which he knew would soon block their path. A hundred yards off to his left, the airship's engines suddenly decreased in intensity as the machine landed. The lights flicked off, plunging them all into darkness. Instinctively, Rex reached up and clicked on his headlamp, which allowed him to see ahead just far enough to make out the wires, which seemed a pale white in the light. To his right, the other two scouts did the same; only Aral moved forward in darkness.

"Come on, faster!" Rex hissed at the others. He couldn't tell what was happening back at the airship, but he assumed that whoever was inside would soon be coming out . . . and after them. Did they have equs, too? Or did they have some other type of machines that would allow them to catch up? Rex cringed at the fact that their headlamps made them into visible targets, but at the same time he was thankful for the ever-thickening guy wires, which kept the deadly aircraft at bay.

Despite his equs's fatigue, he was able to urge the animal to a trot, which was still much faster than a human could run. As the animal pushed deeper into the metallic forest of wires, it seemed to move instinctively, avoiding the metallic obstacles as if with a sixth sense. Rex could only conclude that the equs was used to riding around here and knew how to avoid these tiny obstacles—either that, or it had been trained.

Back where the airship had landed, Rex could hear a volley of shouts and orders. Without looking over his shoulder, he knew that people—Cthonians—had disembarked from the aircraft and were heading their way—though how many, he couldn't tell. By now the airship's engines had fallen silent, and the only other sound on this moonscape was that of the eqūs' snorts and galloping hoof steps.

Rex leaned forward and peered ahead into the darkness beyond the reach of his headlamp. The Power Works' smoldering wreckage was approaching. The wires and stratoneum struts cleared, signaling that he and the others were within one hundred yards of the rubble. As the pile of detritus came into view and the metallic barriers dissolved into the night, Rex recognized the spot where they'd found Aral earlier that day. In the feeble orange light of the remaining fires and the white glare of the three headlamps, Rex could see lingering puddles of acidic water lying stagnant across the ground.

Now all they had to do was turn right and cover the remaining five miles to the pods' wires. Rex pulled the right rein and spurred his eqūs to a faster gallop. The animal complied, though not without snorting and neighing in protest. As the eqūs gained speed, Rex hoped Yoné's and the others' alert signals had not triggered all of the descent pods to climb back up, leaving them stranded. Hopefully there were at least a few remaining . . .

Bam! Bambam!

Rex's heart stopped and his eqūs bolted as sparks exploded from the debris pile to his left. A second later, a high-pitched whizzing zipped in front of his face, while off in the distance the desert spat out geysers of sand ten feet high.

The Cthonians were firing at them.

Bambam!

"Ugh," the two other scouts behind Rex groaned. Without turning around, Rex heard his teammates' bodies slump forward and crash onto the ground. *Beepbeepbeepbeepbeep!* sounded the pods. The only ones now left alive were Rex and Aral.

Consumed with terror, the now rider-less eqūs dashed in front of Rex and disappeared into the night. Rex spurred his own eqūs to run faster. Despite the animal's earlier signs of exhaustion, the eqūs now sensed the danger and mustered a last effort. Rex leaned forward in his saddle and gripped the reins. *Come on, come on, come on . . .* he repeated to himself as the eqūs flew through the dark. Rex's headlamp bobbed and danced across the sand, providing at least a partial glimpse of what lay ahead.

Ziiiiiiiip! A bullet flew by, missing Rex by just a few yards. An instant after the searing metal slug cut through the air, the sound of the gun's report caught up with his ears.

It was quieter than the ones before.

Bambambambam! Ziiiip!

The gunfire was getting farther and farther away. The Cthonians were on foot after all, and they couldn't catch up with the eqūs. Five minutes passed . . . ten. The gunfire faded and faded until it stopped. As the first of the eastern guy wires appeared out of the dark, a wave of relief overcame Rex, despite the terror of the past hour. As long as some of the pods remained, the two of them just might have a chance to escape.

The eqūs slowed.

The guy wires thickened.

The deliberate navigation of the stratoneum forest began again. As they pushed forward, the eqūs too seemed relieved to be able to rest.

"Look! There!" Rex shouted.

Up ahead, the fading rays of his headlamp caused an oblong silhouette to emerge from the dark beyond. The remaining pod. Yoné's. It hadn't gone back up because Rex was the only Ætherian left alive.

"There's only one left," Rex said. His voice was strained with fear, and it faltered as he tried to catch his breath. "It's because of the others. Their pods got the signal they were in trouble, and so . . . "

"What is that?" Aral asked, drawing her eqūs near the descent pod. The Cthonian dismounted and stepped up to the device, inspecting it like a treasure hunter who'd just stumbled upon some lost relic of an extinct civilization.

Seeing Aral next to the pod, Rex was gripped by a new fear.

"Will you—will *we*—even fit in it?" he asked, dismounting. He walked up to the pod. Its hatch remained ajar. Yoné had not closed it completely. "Let's see," he said. He reached forward and opened the hatch, revealing the cushioned seat and the still blinking controls inside.

"I get in?" Aral asked, unconvinced.

"Yes. We both have to fit. You might need to bend your legs, though."

Aral put her hands on either side of the pod's hatch and turned to look over her shoulder. She peered into the distance, back toward the smoldering wreckage of Tátea's Power Works and the remains of the Cthonian outpost, and she squinted her eyes. She held her breath and cocked her head. She then snapped alert.

"They're still coming," she said. "I hear them."

Without hesitating further, she pulled herself up and into the pod. The tall Cthonian worked her way into the seat. Though she stood nearly a full head taller than Rex, she was surprisingly able to wedge herself into the cramped container. To allow her head to fit, she put both knees together and shifted them to one side, as if she were squatting.

"It works," Rex said. He placed his hands on the hatch and pulled himself up. "We'll have to share," he said. He felt his face flush. He knew the only way they could fit would be to ride the entire way with their bodies pressed flat—even squished—against each other.

Aral took a deep breath.

"Well," she said, "there's no other way."

"Right." Rex explained how the pods worked, including what to expect during their passage through the Welcans cloud. He sucked in his chest and wedged himself into the pod. His body squished up against Aral's. He felt her warmth and sweat as the two touched. He could already feel his leg cramping from the strain and awkward angle. Avoiding Aral's eyes, he wiggled around and reached for the hatch. Just before closing it, he turned his head toward the Cthonian. For the first time, he noticed fear in Aral's eyes. She looked back at him and took a deep breath.

"We have to stop this thing," she said.

Rex nodded.

Far off in the night, the sound of a gun popped somewhere in the direction of Tátea's remains.

"Yes, yes, let's go," he snapped, fighting a surge of emotion that was a mixture of terror and despair at having lost not only his father, but also Yoné and the other scouts. Combined with that, here he was in a descent pod with someone who might know his mother—and who might be able to bring them together once more. But here they were, on the brink of war between their two worlds.

Without another word, Rex closed the latch with a click. As the sound of gunfire grew outside, he reached over Aral's head and pressed the small ascent button.

With a clank and a lurch, the overstuffed pod began its slow ascent back to Ætheria.

TWELVE

REX AND ARAL DID NOT TALK.

Each lost in their own terrified thoughts, they both focused on remaining calm as the pod rattled its way up the invisible guy wire outside. Though their faces were less than two inches apart, Rex avoided making eye contact with the Cthonian who held the key to bringing his family together and helping him avert war. He could feel on his face the heat radiating from her cheek, and he could sense the closed space becoming more and more humid as the two filled it with their rapid breaths. Because his back was turned to the blinking control panel, he couldn't tell what their altitude was, never mind what his heart rate or blood-oxygen saturation was. In any case, he wasn't hooked up to the pod's monitors as before, so there was no way he could know anyway.

All he could do was close his eyes and focus on his breathing, with the hope that the small space wouldn't trigger another panic. But here, he wasn't too worried, since he wasn't wearing his SCRM mask. And that was what had triggered his attack earlier. As they mounted, he couldn't tell if the air was becoming thinner, but he knew that when they made it back home, the energizing force of Cthonia's denser air would dissipate.

But what if he could convince the ACF and Deputy Head Schlott that Cthonia's air was not only hospitable, but much more energizing than anything up in Ætheria? Would this be the beginning of a new era of Ætherian development? Would Ætherians look into moving back down to Cthonia's surface?

But right now, there was something more pressing than new settlements: at least some Cthonians thought the Ætherians were trying to kill them, and the Ætherians had the same opinion about the Cthonians. Rex and Aral were the only ones right now who could convince them otherwise. And they had to, or else . . .

Ka-clunk!

The pod lurched and paused in its ascent. The sudden motion pushed Rex's body harder into Aral's, causing them both to miss a breath.

"What was that?" Rex said, looking up as much as the limited space would allow.

"Are we getting close to the cloud?"

Rex nodded. "Must be. It was rough before."

"Hang on."

"Where else would I go?"

Aral let out a stifled chuckle, but it was one that revealed more anxiety than relief. The pod continued its ascent, but Rex soon felt the craft begin to tremble and shake. Outside, the metallic twang of the guy wire's strumming against the pod's surface made him think of a giant guitar. They were entering the cloud, and the higher winds shook them awkwardly against each other. Unlike last time, Rex could hear no rain outside—only wind. As they climbed, he kept his ears alert for any sounds of gunfire from below. By now, they must've been at least a mile up; if the Cthonians were firing, the distance, the wind, and the thick walls of the pod prevented any sounds from reaching his ears.

But then another thought struck: because the two were squeezed in so tightly, what if the pod's hatch had not completely latched? Since they'd started moving, Rex's back had been pushed painfully against the controls and the hatch lever. What if it came open and he fell out? When he'd come down earlier, he'd been strapped in; so that wasn't an issue, even though there was no pressure on the door. But now?

As grim visions of his falling out and through the Welcans cloud spun in his mind, Rex realized that despite his now rapid breathing, he was beginning to feel lightheaded. Trying to calm himself, he took in large gulps of air, only to feel as though he hadn't breathed at all. Inches away, he noticed that Aral was opening her mouth wider to take in air.

They were entering the stratosphere. They were leaving the thick Cthonian air behind.

And then Rex wondered: was Aral okay? She'd never been this high, and her body wasn't used to breathing air this thin. Panic struck: What if she passed out? Became hypoxic? Died? And all because Rex hadn't had the foresight to find a SCRM mask for her. But how could he have? At the time, their only goal had been to escape the gunfire from below.

"Are you okay?" he asked.

Aral nodded.

"I just have to breathe deeper. That's all. But there are two of us in here, and we're using up the air. Hopefully not much longer."

Rex thought. She was right. Maybe she wasn't

reacting to the thinner air after all, but to the increased carbon dioxide that the two of them were filling the descent pod with. He breathed in deeply and felt as though he was short of breath. Yes, that must be it. He grew up in Ætheria, after all, and so breathing at altitude had never been a problem for him. Perhaps she'd be fine. After all, he was sure that it had been the cold that had killed those other Cthonians, and not the lack of oxygen. Or at least he tried to convince himself of that . . .

The shaking ceased. The humming vibrations of the guy wire stopped. Their ride became smooth once more. They were above the Welcans cloud.

The closer their pod rose toward Ætheria, a new sensation crept into Rex's body. For the first time since descending with the other scouts, he realized he was wracked with anxiety about everything that he'd seen and discovered since his descent: the truth about Cthonia's air, the truth about the attack, and what was now a massive responsibility for him and Aral to let the Ætherian government know. His world was beginning to fall apart, and he was just beginning to understand that he was one of the only ones who could stop it. And to add to all of this, here he had a clue as to the whereabouts of his mother, whose face he'd seen only as a baby.

Bam!

The pod lurched to a stop. A spurt of adrenaline radiated from Rex's chest and into his arms and legs.

Something hard and rigid bumped into the pod from the outside. In an instant, Rex could feel that the pod was no longer free to sway on the guy wire. Amid metallic clanks and scratches, the pod jiggled its way up what felt like a track or guiding rails. They had arrived. They were being pulled up and into Island Twenty-Three's warehouse. Rex was covering the same path he'd done just under twenty-four hours ago, but now in reverse.

Still not speaking, Rex and Aral tried as best they could to brace themselves against the sides of the pod, without relying too much on each other's bodies for support. With one final jolt, the pod shot up about four feet and then flopped onto its back. The hatch was now facing up, and Rex was lying on Aral, who groaned under the new weight.

"Ugh."

"Sorry, sorry, sorry, sorry . . . " Rex tried to wiggle around and push himself up and off of her as much as he could, but the pod's hatch kept him firmly pressed against her.

"Just stop moving," she said. "Just stop." She kept her face turned away from his. She seemed to be struggling for air and focusing intently on keeping calm. A thin layer of sweat coated her features.

"Yeah," he muttered, gasping.

Clank!

The pod came to a complete stop.

And in the next second, the pressure flew from Rex's back as the hatch was ripped open. Frigid air stung Rex's exposed skin: his head, his neck, his hands. As his body chilled, he suddenly became aware of how sweaty he was and how hot and humid the two had been in the cramped pod.

Before he could react, what felt like dozens of hands rained down on him, grabbing at his arms, his shoulders, his legs, his hands. The hands clamped down and lifted him from the pod with such force that it seemed that whoever was lifting him assumed he couldn't move on his own. As he was lifted up and away from Aral, he noticed that her hair was drenched and covering her face. She gasped in relief as Rex's weight was removed from her stomach.

As for Rex, the hands set him on his feet and withdrew. He tensed his exhausted leg muscles to keep from falling over. He held his arms out to steady himself. His head still spun, but he couldn't tell if it was from the sudden lack of oxygen, from the overwhelming emotion of everything he'd experienced, or a combination of both. The lights of the hangar blinded him, and a roar of voices engulfed him in a swirl of noise.

He blinked. He wiped his eyes. He looked around. And what he saw was a scene of utter panic.

Behind him, Aral had stood straight up, stretching to her superhuman height. She stretched her legs and right arm, revealing her full size. Her eyes scanned the room before settling on Rex's. A glint of understanding flashed across her pupils, but this quickly faded as the crowd of ACF gasped and recoiled as if she had been some giant, deadly snake.

"Oh, my God!"

"They've come up!"

"A spy!"

"It's one of them!"

"They're here! It's happening!"

Screams erupted through the hanger. Some of the ACF troops ran, while others looked around with imploring eyes. No one came within twenty feet of the Cthonian, who stepped out of the pod and began walking toward Rex. Her eyes betrayed the fear that now gripped her in this foreign environment. She furrowed her brow and looked imploringly at Rex. Rex immediately noticed that she didn't look well: her skin had become paler than normal, and she seemed clammy. She opened and closed her mouth like a fish out of water, as if gasping for air.

Oh, my God, Rex thought. *Can she even breathe up here?!*

"No!" Rex screamed, trying to project his voice over the growing din. But even he was still unaccustomed to the lack of oxygen, and his vocal cords didn't respond to his effort. Only a few others heard his cry. He reached out and took a step forward, but someone pulled him back. Rex turned and stood face-to-face with Deputy Head Schlott, whom he hadn't noticed in the chaos.

"Stop!" Schlott screamed, her eyes shooting to Aral. She dug her fingers into Rex's shoulder, pulling him back. "Stop that Cthonan! Arrest her! And you . . . " She shifted her fiery gaze to Rex. But before she could say anything else, the two of them were swarmed by a throng of ACF scouts, who bombarded Rex with questions. As they spoke, Rex tried to wrench himself free from Schlott's grip. He stood on his toes to peer over the others' shoulders. Among all of the heads, shoulders, and arms moving about, he saw that Aral too had been surrounded by ACF scouts, who were pressing in on her.

"Are you okay?"

"What happened to the others?"

"Where is your mask?"

"Did the others suffocate?"

"What's going on?!"

Voices erupted around Rex—so many that he couldn't identify who was saying what. The hangar was filled with people, far more than when he'd last seen it, fewer than twenty-four hours ago.

With vision still slightly blurred from exhaustion and the sudden shift in temperature that stung his face, he looked around. Off to his right, dozens of ACF recruits swarmed around Aral like ants pouring over a carcass. He could no longer see her face or body, but he knew she was there. At the center of the room, men and women leaned in and plunged their hands into every nook and cranny of the now-open descent pods, pressing buttons, pulling out wires, checking connections. Everyone seemed to be talking at once.

"Rex?" Schlott said in a loud voice. She squeezed his arm to get his attention. He turned around and faced her. "We need to talk. Now."

Rex nodded.

"Yes, of course," he said, "but . . . " Schlott's eyes were narrowed almost to slits. She seemed to be fighting off conflicting emotions: worry, confusion, anger, and soldierly determination. Under her withering gaze, Rex couldn't finish his sentence. His mind raced with everything he needed to tell Schlott. He felt the urgency to act, to do something, to stop any more people—Ætherian or Cthonian—from losing their lives because of some stupid misunderstanding.

"The air," Rex continued, his voice squeaking from panic. "We *can* breathe down there. On Cthonia, I mean. It's even better than here," his voice faded into a mumble as the biting cold worked its way into his jaw, slowing his speech.

"What's that?" Schlott widened her eyes and stepped back.

"We don't *need* masks, is what I'm saying. I'm telling you, it's harder for me to breathe here than . . . "

A noise behind Rex cut him off. He whirled around. Schlott tightened her grip. It was not a kind, friendly squeeze. It was one of an iron grip meant to keep Rex from moving. Rex grimaced almost imperceptibly and tried to work his shoulder free. But Schlott squeezed harder.

"Look!" Rex said, now pointing at the crowd of ACF that were struggling around Aral. *What were they doing? Was she still standing? Or had she collapsed?* Some of the scouts were leaning over, as if she'd fallen to the floor. Rex looked back at Schlott, his eyes imploring. "*She'll* tell you. She helped us. We've got to do something. It's all wrong. I mean, we've got it all wrong . . . "

As Rex spoke, he realized that his words were becoming garbled. His brain overflowed with thoughts—most of them panicked—and the thoughts were colliding into each other as they tried to rush through his mouth at the same time. He thought of everything that had happened: of Yoné's and the others' deaths, of the collapse of Tátea's Power Works, and of his mother, whom Aral seemed to know . . .

"What's that?" Schlott asked.

"She is not an enemy," Rex repeated. "And she knows my mom! Please!"

"Enough!" Schlott snapped, the veins bulging in her temples. She looked at the ACF scouts that surrounded them. "Take that Cthonian girl to the holding facility on Island Twenty. She knows something, and we can't let her free until we find out what!"

Schlott released her grip, and the ACF troops descended upon Aral.